AF484004

LEEPORDER AND THE FORBIDDEN UNIVERSES

despite of the bright moon is normal.
Bu the underworld see it as the   calling to take lives.
It was a silent night on the street of Navarre, and in the street sat
a sewer in the middle of the road.   it was around 12:oo
and that's when the moons   come out.   they was wearing
shadow black and colorful hairs, and   also use   black magic
to   prey on their victims who wanted
out   because it gives the moon life to hear, Talk, see,
and to make commands what-ever it like.
A group of teens was sitting around a camp-fire telling stories,
until five goth moons   appear out of the fire.
''That was creepy as hell!   Said a female. As she was smiling.
''What   this, some kind of trick, Its not Halloween, losers!
Shouted a teen boy with blonde hair. tossing a drink in the
Moons face.   Suddenly, one of the moons bite into his
neck and stone him to death.   The teens runs for their
lives   but the moons block their path with demons and

stone the teens. ''This is so boring'' I want something hard to get'' Said Debbie. We can try a church! Said Dablo. As he licks the blood off the knife and enters the fire.

A catholic church was located in the middle of nowhere , and four monks
guarded each side of the church. As the church was in service.
The ground opens and fire burns the monks
to death and others as well.   Next, the door fly open
to a pope sitting in a chair, holding a long staff.
He was an old fat man, wearing glasses. he's confident
with a cocky attitude.   The members of the church
stares out of curiosity,   As the moons walk down
the aisle.   "Sitting in this church', wont save you!
Said Kasey. 'Would you please bless me father?

Said omen. As he approach the pope and takes a knee. The pope
give him a weird stare and grip   the center of his staff.
Aren't you gonna bless me father?? Omen asked. What do you want?
Asked the pope.   As he try to strike Omen. You wasn't gonna strike
me father weren't you?'' Omen asked.   Catching the staff with his
hand and snatch it from him.

next, he slash his throat.   The people run to the door and it
was jammed. 'The orange moon' is almost full!!!!
shouted Omen. As he take up his staff and burn the whole
 entire church .   { A woman took her little brother for
a walk, until   Omen   step out of the tree.
Nice! to see you again. Said Omen.
I already told you im out! Said Jenny.   As she grab her
brother and start walking.   the other three block her path.
So she take her brother and walk across the street.
As her heart start to race and her brother had no clue
what was going on.
Give up bitch! you're not getting away! Said Kasey. Pulling the
knife out of her pocket. " Don't kill her". Said Omen. Run! Shouted
Jenny.
As she push one of the moon's.   Toby got away
and Jenny was push against the tree and wrap in fire ropes.
It burn!   It burn!   One thing you have to under-stand is….
To get out of the moon's, you have to die! Said Omen. As
the rope of fire burn Jenny alive and the

Moons ful-fill the orange moon, by making one last visit.
{Jimmy is a punk-rock singer who use to be a former
moon, causing him'self to speed down the free-way
with a group of guys in a four door car. Jimmy rocks
his head, to Heavy music and shouting at the public.
"Born to be wild!!!! shouted three of the guys, who road
in the back-seat. "Im no'longer a moon!! shouted Jimmy.

Suddenly, Kacey land on the hood and Jimmy hit the brakes.
Kacey?? he asked. "Long time no see" Said Kacey.
Giving him a   flirty smile,   and showing half of her leg.

8

Jimmy exit the car, and she jump of the hood, smiling evil.
How come you're still a moon?   Jimmy asked.
Kacey walk up to Jimmy and said, the only way out
is death, and she cut his throat. including
his friends . "Didnt know you was so charming!''
Said Omen. Meet me at the bridge!'' Spoke the orange moon.
With a proud tone in his voice.

So the moons gathered at the bridge and stood before the orange moon.
"We come before you! Said Omen.   "You all done a great job!''

CHAPTER : 2

The moon replied.   Approaching from the left side of the bridge,
a gothic woman, with green and black short hair.
" nice to see you again" Said Omen.   I want out! Shouted Julie.
How dare you! Said Kacey.   The deal is already done and your
soul is on the line! Omen said. Julie try walking away, and
the moons block her. " Only death" Said the orange moon.

Julie look confused.

Get her! Said Omen. The moons ambush Julie aggressive'ly
 until a woman appear, dressed in an old 1700"s western
dress, and carry's a latern. she throws it at the moons,
causing them to run away. Are you ok? She asked Julie.
Julie looks at her, and fainted. "Nice to see you Cindy!
Spoke the moon. You work for Saltin and had them to kill people
for power and life! Said Cindy. "Its the only way we feed from!
The moon said. Cindy swing her lantern, and throw
it at the moon, and it become bright again.   The lantern comes back,

and change into a door. Suddenly, a car was coming down the road.
 Swiftly, Cindy removes Julie, and enters the door, and vanish.
The man hit the brake , and get out of the car.
The door was already gone. As he approach further up the road.
Next, he look over the bridge and see nothing.
I must be seeing things! He said. "Leaving him curious."
Julie   woke   up   and saw spirits standing over her.
Swiftly, she rolls to the other side, and fall' out of bed. We wont
hurt you! One of them spoke.   Who are you?! Julie asked.
We are good spirits! Said   the voice of a male.
Julie gets up and run out of the room, and   appear in a office.
"Im so glad you're okay! Spoke a man, who' work' at the
desk, and from the 1400's.   Julie touch her head, and
body, and feels no pain. Where am I?!" Julie asked.
"The white kingdom, of The after life! He said. Wait, Im dead??

Julie asked. "Its just the name, and you're much alive.
He replied. Who are you and how do you know all of this?
Julie asked. "You may call me Sr. Gabe! and I am also the

13

keeper of the kingdom. Said Gabe. Gently, fixing his neck-tie.
{The moons returns back to the sewer, and sat around the pool of
blood. You all did well! Said Pitts. As he's a dark priest,
and the master of all. Cindy came! Said Kacey. We had to run.
Said Omen. she's too powerful". Pitt's replied. What shall we
do? Kacey asked. Send out more demons, to cause more death's".
Said Pitts. As he puts his left hand over the tub of blood,
and 300 demons was being created.
With pig heads, and nun's. they're ugly!! shouted Kacey.
"Their bodies are made out of mist". Said Omen.
I want you all to go and destroy all good! I'll make you
stronger! Said Pitts. Suddenly, the demons make's a loud growl,
 and travel through earth's ground. {Gabe shows Julie, the most
famous shops.

CHAPTER : 3

15

"Whats that shop?! Asked Julie. When you become a warrior, you'll
get your weaponds from there! Said Gabe.
{Julie approach a Bakery shop because she saw cup-cakes and cookies.
 Something you like?' Gabe asked.   These cup-cake's look delicious!
Julie said. Lets go in! Gabe said. Holding the door
open for Julie. Where you from?'' Asked a fat lady who was
glowing white. Im from pennsylvania! Said Julie. You must
be a special person to come in this kingdom!' Said the fat
lady. As she put on gloves- that was golden. She would like a

cup-cake! Said Gabe. "Pick anything you want for free'' She said
to Julie. I have no money! to give you. Julie said
 money's not allow! Said Gabe. Julie give's them both
a stare! Thats for the world you came from!
Said the fat lady. So how do you   receive payments from
customers?'' Julie asked.   Its free! She said to Julie. " Miss
Shell is right'' Said Gabe. "I would like three cookies!
and three cup-cakes! Said Julie. At your service! Shell said.

So Gabe and Julie exit the shop and continues their detour.
Julie reache' in her bag and give   Gabe a cup-cake.
Thank you!   Said Gabe. As Julie eats the cookie.

The demons had made their way to earth and created their own nest
to cause death on each mission. rain pours,
on a crazy home that sat a-long side of the woods.
and   also covered in the dark, lone'ly silent night.
No car's insight - unless family members comes
to see their love ones. One of the staff members walks out
for a smoke and his name is Matt. Big temper and mexican
body builder and tats all over him.   If these people dont
shut up! I'll kill them all.! I love your thinking..!"
said a voice. who's there? Matt asked.   in the rain!"
The voice replys. Matt looks through the rain and
the demon jumps into his body and enters the building.
there's a woman who wont shut up! Linda said to Matt.
As she was the head of the staff. I'll go take care of

it! said Matt. As he take out his bat and approach the room.
I'll eat your blood!! She screams. Matt opens the door
and started beating her to death. Blood splats all over the
room and matt closed the door and walks away.
Linda walks down the hall and opens the door to only see
the patient dead. Next time, you'll be silent! Said Linda.
As she closed the door. Let this be a warning to all of you!
If you make any noise or misbehave, you'll be beat!
Linda shouted.

A man name Leeporder, heard the message of Linda and sits back
in his seat. they're hurting people? Lee asked him'self.
Lee was believed to be put in the crazy home because of
his gifted ways and some say he knew too much .
Lee has black short hair and he's tall. His room was a
master room where he has a fridge, bed, desk couch and a
computer.   Lee finish sixty page's of his life story.
Another female in her 30's, was to believed to be put in the
crazy home because of stealing and violence's.   Heather

is a tom-girl with long blonde hair and blue eyes. She also
18

has a master bed-room like Lee's. Suddenly, the doors opens.
As it was time for lunch. Lee and Heather comes out at
the same time. "Who let you out?! She asked?
"The magic key you have! Said Lee. All of you get in line!
Shouted Linda. As guards approaches.

Heather become worried! As she didnt see her best-friend. Where's
Candy? Heather asked. she's dead! Linda said.
Suddenly, Heather run's to her door, and see's blood all over
the room. One of the guards "strike Heather in her back.

CHAPTER : 4

21

{Julie sat on a bench and eat the rest of her cookies and so
did Gabe. "How come you didnt get any?"
Julie asked. Too much sweets are very bad! Said Gabe.
You ate one of my cup-cakes! Said Julie. "That was a one
time thing! Said Gabe. You must be new in town?
Asked a black cow-boy and he was in his mid 30's. "Im from
earth and whats your name? Julie asked. Call me Lamar!
and this is my friend skippy. Said Lamar. What a funny name!
Said Julie. Skippy spits and smiles. "You never spit
infront of a lady. Said Lamar. It was a welcome spit! Said
Skippy. "Try not to do it again! Said Lamar. Im sorry Julie!

Some times we dont think!" Said Gabe. So, what do you do on
earth? Lamar asked. Well... I was with the moons for a
long time and I told them I wanted out! so they started
jumping me. Said Julie. Sound like a group thing!

Said Skippy. Indeed! and Cindy saved me." Said Julie. you're
22

lucky that Cindy saved you or, you wouldnt be here! Said Lamar.
I owe her my life! Said Julie. As a team! Said Lamar.
Look like you're one of us! Said Skippy. If you went back to
earth, they'll kill you; Said Gabe. I want to be strong like
you guys! Said Julie.   What make's you think we're
strong? Lamar asked.   You both have weaponds and ready
to fight! Julie Replys. "she's real good! Said Skippy.
I must get back! Said Gabe. As he take's his cane
and hits the ground twice and vanish.   Whoa!!!!!!
shouted Julie. "Amazing! huh? Lamar asked. " Shocked me!
when I first came here! Said Skippy.   When did you get
here? Julie asked. Lets get you to the court-yard and I'll

tell you on the way." Said Skippy. As he spits - again.
{Heather sits next to a black lady with braids in her hair;
and she gossiped about the food she was eating.
Cant believe they're making us eat this slop! She said to
Heather. Meal is better than no meal Lisa! Said Heather.
Oh! now you're their slave! Shouted Lisa. Keep your voice
down" Heather said. As a guard was looking around.
Lisa takes her tray and throws it and everyone else did the
same. Lee and Heather finish eating. As the rest
was beating and dragged away. "wise for the both
of you to not throw your trays" Said the cafe.
When are we leaving here? Heather asked. Another seven
years! She said to Heather. Leeporder shakes his head.

After they ate, Lee and Heather was sent to the entertainment room.

Lee sat by the window, and play cars to him'self. Can I join
you? Heather asked" with a smile. Only none pretty girls
allow! Said Lee. Please..? Heather asked. Alright, Have a
seat! Said Lee. Heather sit in the chair, thats across
from Lee and look out the window. Beautiful, isnt
it? Lee asked. I think about becoming a bird, every-day - in my life!
Said Heather. What brings you here? Lee asked.
Stealing and other things! Heather Replied. You seem like a
fun person! Said Lee. Suddenly, the chairs start
shaking and they both jumps up and run
to the door. Next, the lights start laughing and
flickering. Whats going on? Heather asked. both
security's start searching the room until, three demons
jumps into their bodies , and turns towards
Lee and Heather. Whats going on? Asked Linda. Something's
wrong with your guards! Said Lee. You wouldnt
try to escape, would you? Linda asked. Frowning at the both of them.

Swiftly, Lisa tackels Linda to the floor and start punhing
her. Run!!! she shouted. Heather and Lee runs out the room.
As they both hold hands .

{Julie stood before Cindy and other warriors after her.
They wanted you dead; Said Cindy. My heart wasnt made
for that. and I dont want to hurt people! Said Julie.
You thought they was some goth people who was cool,
and you didnt know what you was getting your-self into.
Cindy Replied. Teach me to be strong! Julie said. That's
why you're here! Cindy said. "Julie smiles. Should I show?
Lamar asked. Cindy throw four roses in the sky, and Lamar

jump   off the ground and shoot at the roses and land

on feet. "That was sick!!   Julie shouted. oh...hes just showing
off! Said Skippy. As he take;s off his badge and throws
it at the roses and the kingdom shook for 3' sec short.
"I told you that was forbidden". Said Cindy. I forgot"
Skippy Replied. "The other warriors start laughing.
I dont see you doing nothing! Said Skippy.
"You have to blame your-self" Said Lamar. Can you fly?
Cindy asked Julie.   I cant fly, im a human! Julie said.

CHAPTER : 5

you' just limit your-self! Cindy said. What am I suppose
to say? Julie asked.   You can fly." Cindy said.
"I can fly! Said Julie. "You have to believe. Said Lamar.
Julie close her eyes and said… I can fly!   Suddenly, her
 feet lift off the ground and land' back down. Did you see that???!
Julie asked. Well, done! Said Cindy. As three roses and a
bow and arrow, appear to her in the color of
silver and black. "These are so beautiful!   Cried" Julie.
You can take this everywhere , on your journey.   Said Cindy.

The world shouldnt see . Said Lamar. What if they did?
Julie asked. It will banish you. Lamar. Replied.
You have my word! Said Julie.   As she pick up the bow
and arrow, and shoot at the bush'es. "Use one
of these before? Skippy asked. My uncle owns one!
Said Julie. You must enter the next yard". Said Cindy. Julie

proceed to the next yard and there was an Asian man, standing with   the   hands, behind the back and wearing a white robe.

{every now and then, the moons partied, and drank blood
and some even wash their face with it. When are we ready?
Omen asked. What do you want? Pitts asked.
As he sat in a high seat, chair.   When do we find a new location?
Omen asked. we cant be exsposed". Pitts said.
It can be in the middle of nowhere. Omen said.
Walking around pits – and drinking a cup of Blood.
When the time is right! Pitts Said. How about you and I have
some fum? Omen asked Any plans? Pitts
 asked. Lets go mess with the hospital! Said Omen. " Im up

for it! Said Pitts. As he get out of the chair.
{Julie was trip on her back. You have to get up more swiftly!

Said Chow!.   Aint no way to treat a lady! Said Julie.
As she   {attack}   Chow..
The chow dodge and push Julie with his shoulder.
I see Chow is given you a wonderful lesson! Said Cindy.
"he's starting to get on my nerve's! Said Julie. As
she charge at him, and chow knock her down
with his powers. Too much anger" Said Chow. As he help
Julie up, with his powers.   you're cheating! Julie shouted.
"Things cant be easy for you! Chow said. In a play'ful tone.

Julie   becomes angry, until she used
her arms to block his powers. Chow went backwards.
Great job!" said Cindy. You passed the first test! Now,
you must learn to fight" Said Chow. As he strikes Julie
down. Julie brave'ly gets back up, and block
his strike's and kicks him down. Chow smile's
and bows to Julie. Is it over? Julie asked. Not yet!
Said Chow. As he set up three flower dummy's.

{Pitts and Omen, arrive at the Hospital and they both wears
red. Can I help you two? Asked the nurse, working at
the front desk.   We want lives. Said Pitts.   If something
wromg with you, I can have you seen!" She said.

Pitts take's up his nail and slash the nurse's throat
and become's dead. As she fall's out of the chair.
Every-body in the hospital, becomes shocked!.   Freeze!
Shouted security. As both   approach Pitts and
Omen, and started searching them Both. Pitts slash the first
security in the eyes, and Omen slash the second one.

Next, Pitts sealed the Entrance with blood; as the people
run' for their lives.   Where are you human's going?!
Omen asked?   As objects started   attacking   them,
and doors closing. Whats going on? Asked the doctor.
As he come out with a tool in his hand.
Suddenly, Omen grab the doctor by his jacket and throw him
against the wall, and more doctors came running out-
and Pitts and Omen start attacking them all.   But , there
was one beautiful nurse name Joana, and she's spanish with a

slender body and brown hair. She see the doctors
and nurses, battling paranormal men, and some
of them was being killed. Suddenly, the lights shut
off and a huge growl approach. Joana half -way close
the door, and what she saw   was " desturbing." demons
running on their backs and some on   their hands. She shut the
door silent'ly.

{Julie becomes ready, as her training was completed. She then take a knee. "you're ready" Said Chow.
Some hospital is under-attack!   Shouted one of the warriors.
As he was a male with blonde hair and a
soilder from the 1915"s, and carried a gun on his right shoulder. You must be from the old'en days! Said Julie.
"Yes, and way before your time! He said.
This is Zack, firearms. he fights for the kingdom!"
Said Cindy. What are we gonna do about the situation? Asked Skippy. "You and Lamar go check it out. Said Chow.
Lamar and Skippy runs over to a light pole and touch'es it".
All of a sudden; they vanish. "Julie rub her eyes. As she was in "disbelief! It's a short way to earth" Said Zack. This got

to be heaven! Said Julie. "still wouldnt be your time" Said Cindy.

CHAPTER : 6

Lamar and Skippy arrive at the front entrance of the Hospital. As blood block their paths. How are we suppose to

get through?
Skippy asked. "You cant let evil win" Said Lamar.
As he take out his shot-gun. and shoot the blood
and it melts like ice. "I'll give you credit for the job!
Said Skippy. As they both enter the Hospital and see' everyone
dead.   "Nice for you to drop in".
said Pitts. What did you do to these people? Skippy asked.
"We wanted lives and they played hero". Said Omen.
This Hospital doesnt belong to either of you! So leave!
Shouted Lamar. "That wont be happening". Pitts Replied. As the
demons start approaching. " Its only two of us". Said Skippy.
 Life isn't fair". Said Omen. Kill them!!
shouted Pitts. Lamar and Skippy, jump behind the desk and

start shooting . "This is easy stuff". Said Skippy. As
he spits and pull out a second gun. Omen look at Pitts.

"Just let them have their fun". Said Pitts. As he cross his arms
infront of him. Swiftly, Joana throw' salt on the both of
them and run. Omen and Pitts chase after her. you're gonna
pay for that!}} Said Omen. As he slide on his feet and two

other demons behind him.
{Lee and Heather found rain coats and throw them on.
Next, they runs   out the entrance door.
Where are you two!!?   Linda Shouted. Gone! Said Jeff. As

he was carrying a knife, with blood on it. Linda walks out the
Entrance and scans with her eyes. "Theres no-where for them to go".
Linda said. "Only in the woods.
Said Jeff. Indeed". Lets gather some weapons!   Linda
said. So Lee and Heather kept running, until they see' a house.
Hold it!   What are you two doing on my land? Asked
an older woman. As she points a shot-gun at them.
Her hair was long and grey, and wearing a grey dress.
Look, someone's after us and we need help! "Cried" Heather.
 people dress like that, comes from the crazy home!

CHAPTER : 7

She said. We're victim's." Said Lee. The lady lower' her gun. Come inside! She said.

{On the other side of pennsylvania, sat a small police department, and only two cops was on night shift. A female name Angela, who's a Fbi and another male cop name Scott. they've   ordered pizza and watched an old film called, ghost and mr chicken. Angela has long black hair and round face, with a confident attitude. Scott is a beta type guy, with orange hair and wear's glasses. Angela puts her hair in a pony tail.   As she was eats pizza. Suddenly, the power goes off. " that' never happened". Said Angela. "I'll go check it out". Said Scott. As he get out of the chair and walk

outside. { as "The fuse box was only around the corner.}
When Scott made it to the destination, there he see a beautiful

44

nun, standing by the fuse box. Please!.. step away from the box.
Said Scott. "aint no way to talk to a lady! She said.
Why are you messing with the fuse box? Scott asked.

Suddenly, the nun put her head down and start crying.
"I have no brain, and I need help!" she cried.
Scott lower his gun, and walk towards her. The nun hug him.
 Lets take you inside the
station! Said Scott. All of a sudden, the nun dig her nails into his
skin, and open her mouth and swollow
his whole body. leaving no trace. Angela gets up and walk
outside, and Scott was nowhere to be found. Where the heck
are you?

Angela shouted. As she see' the fuse box and turn on the power.
Next, she look around for Scott and still, no sign of him.
So she turn around, and walks back to the department.
As soon as she entered The Department, there she see a nun sitting
in her chair, staring at her. Have you seen a officer name
Scott? Angela asked. The nun shake her head yes.
Where? Angela asked. "I ate him". The nun said.. "Thats impossible."
Angela said. Suddenly, the nun throw up Scotts body
and Angela draw her gun. you're suppose to be under God!!
Shouted Angela. What god are you talking about?
The nun asked. As her eyes start falling out and she stand up.

Angela shoot at her, and the nun laughs. Next, Angela
run out The Department. " Why are you running? The nun
asked. Walking to the door.   Angela jump into the
car and drive off.   "You cant run forever! Said the Nun. As she

as she vanish from the Department, and start jumping from tree to tree. Angela look through the rear mirror, and see the nun jumping from tree to tree. When Angela drove across the bridge, the nun stop. "Why did she stop? Angela "thought to her'self."

 The nun Appear, and flip the car over and Angela passe's out.
Next, The nun rip the door off, and drag Angela s body
out of the car and open her mouth.   Angela shoots the nun
and sits up. The nun turn into blood and sink
into the crack of the street. "Angela couldnt believe what was

happening". The radio was broke, and a man from the bakery shop
comes running out. " Are you ok, Officer?   As he was a
middle weight man with short black hair. "Going somewhere?

asked the voice, coming from the tree. Get inside!!" Shouted Angela. As her and the bakery runs in at the same time and Angela lock the door. Can you call for back up? He asked. I cant go back to The Departmen't and my car's damage". Angela Replied. they're here for death!

Said an old skinny lady who's 60 years old and has grey short hair. Not now, Aunt Joe! He said. You bought a cop in our shop, Benny? Joe asked. " Look, theres something out there! Said Angela. Yes, and its after you!!! shouted Joe. Its after all of us!. Angela said. You need to leave our shop.! Joe shouted. I said she can stay!! shouted Benny. Joe walk towards the door and unlocks it. Next, she open it. I can let them inside!! said Joe. What are you doing?? Benny asked. Letting "whats after her in". said Joe. Benny run to her rescue: as the nun grab joe

49

CHAPTER : 8

by the neck, and try to pull her out the door. Angela shoot at
the nun, from a far distance and The nun release Joe.
How dare that thing grab me? Joe asked. I could let it!
Angela said. I didnt need your help anyway!! Joe said.
You owe her your life: Aunt Joe! Said Benny. Joe walks
away, with-out a response. Do you have a phone?
Angela asked. Over there on the wall!" Benny said.
The cord's been cut. Said Angela.
{Just then, "it was time for Julie to leave the White-kingdom.
"your Journey A-waits you, and you may take as many
party members, as you wish"! Cindy said.
I'll take Zack, Gabe, Skippy" and Lamar" Said Julie.
May my blessings be with you all!" said Cindy. As she hug
Julie. Goodbye Cindy" said Zack. leaving

.

her sight. "Lets go and tell Gabe". Said Zack. As him and
Julie both, touch the light pole and vanish. Joana come to
a dead end. As the Entrance was blocked off. "there's nowhere
to run now.! Said Pitts. Joana turn towards

Omen and there was more than one her, and start dancing.
As they wears white dresse's. Suddenly, white spirits
charge at them with swords in their hands, and start "attacking.

Lamar and Skippy, kill all the demons and see' Joana
in trouble. Pitts flee, by running away. Omen vanish as
well. Leaving the demons to fight. The spirits finish
off the demons, and return back into Joanas body.
"You okay? Asked Lamar. Yes , and who are you two, and why
did they attack this Hospital? Joana asked. My names Lamar,
and this is my partner Skippy." Said Lamar. Thats a funny name!
Joana said. "My mother gave me the name because I would
always get in trouble! Said Skippy. " Do you have to tell
this story again? Lamar asked. Later". I have to check on these

People. Said Joana. As she run where the cops was. When she look back, they was gone. See anyone you know? One of the cops asked. no! Joana said. {Alright! Is everyone ready? Gabe asked. As everyone was packed in a 1959 car that

was all black and white. "What they for? Julie asked.
"Put on your seat belt, and I'll show you. Gabe said..
Putting his hand on the center gear. " Im ready! Said Julie.
Suddenly, Gabe pull the gear back and off the car went in
full speed. Julie hold' on for dear life. "you'll get use to it".

CHAPTER : 9

Zack. {Lee and Heather had changed into new clothing. As the
old ones was thrown away. Lee wears sport blue shorts,
with a white t-shirt and running shoes. Heather wears pink
jeans, with a pink top, and a base-ball cap backwards.

"Thanks for letting us use your shower! Said Heather. " Come and
eat. She said to the both of them. { So Heather and Lee sit at
the table, eating and telling their stories.}   "Heather look over
at Lee and smiles. I use to be one of their patients". She
said. "What's your name? Heather asked. Betty!
Said Betty. a sprear was throwed   through the window and

lands in her head. Lee and Heather jumps from the table , and
start locking the doors. "I know you're in there!!   shouted Linda.
As ten guards surrounds the house, carrying
silver bats. Lee look around for him and Heather to escape.

Suddenly, he see a basement door. Throw the fire bottles, boys!!!
Linda shouted. Run to the basement door. Said Lee.
As he runs for the door and enters first, and then Heather.
Bottles of fire was being throwed through the windows
and the house start burning. What are we gonna do?
Heather asked. suddenly, Lee saw a tall lamp and it was
lit bright. Do you see that? Lee asked. Yes, I do.
Heather said. As the both of them approach the Lamp.

"It must lead to some where! Said Lee. Swiftly, smoke spreads
inside the basement and their eyes start burning. Lets touch
it. said Lee. At the same time, they both touch it and ended
up in a -nother world. "Such clean white streets, and buildings!

"welcome, to the White-kingdom.! Said Cindy. Who are you? Heather

Asked. "My name is Cindy" and im the owner of this kingdom".
Said Cindy. "We had trouble". Said Lee. Linda is
after you both, and Betty's dead. Said Cindy. How did you know

that? Heather asked. "Betty use to be a long time warrior and she wanted to be normal again, and I gave her her wish! Cindy said. Can you help us? Lee asked. Indeed! Cindy

CHAPTER : 10

Replys.
{Jessica is gothic, and born a witch.   Her mother
is a witch and her father's mortal.   Jessica has long black
hair and pale white face and she's wearing a long blue and
black dress, with blue combat boots.   Her house was the
lonely house on the block.   As the others houses was straight

down.   Jessicas house was surrounded by black gates and black
horses.   Two drunk men, decided to disturb her
peace. So one of them throw a glass bottle through her window.
"Come out you creepy witch! he shouted. why did you
throw a bottle through my window?   Jessica asked.
"Because I want to have a date with you". He said to Jessica.

Jessica telepath's from her room to the gate. "Im way too mystic
for you." Jessica said. As she pulls his face through the gate ,
and punch out his heart. Two of the other men pulls
out a knife and Jessica burns it out of their hands,
and pulls their bodie's through the gate. Causing their bodie's to
break in-half - Leaving no trace of ashes or blood.
Jessica calmly   walks away. "You have mail! Said the mail
man. Swiftly, Jessica reach out and the mail comes
to her. Have a great day! Said the mail- man. As he drives
off into the distance.

"I have to go to the store". Said Jessica. As she gets on the black
horse and the gate open, and she ride off into the distance.
People of the block stops what they are doing, to stare at her.

{Gabe and Julie, arrives at the other side of pennsylvania and a nun was hit. I.. think you hit someone". Said Zack.
Gabe get out of the car, to only see a nun laying on the ground..

my dear boy, you was right! "We did hit a nun! Said Gabe.
Suddenly, the nun put her claw through Gabe's chin
and he vanish. Julie jump out the car and shoot
the nun. Zack get out of the car and draw out his gun.
Gabe is gone! Cried Julie. He wants us to keep fighting.
Said Zack. Angela look out the window and see'
Zack and Julie, and she run out-side.   Can you help us??
 Angela asked. Zack and Julie runs over to
Angela, in a helpful way. Whats wrong? Julie asked.
My partner was killed by this nun and I took off running
for my life, and I ended up meeting these people!!
Calm down, we know they're evil. Said Zack. What is your
name? Asked Julie. My name's Angela! Angela said.

"My name's Julie and this is Zack". Julie said.   Suddenly, Benny
and Joe screams and the three of them went running. Before

they enters the building, it explode and they all was knock down. Angela becomes shocked". As the face of a beast start laughing, and looks around swiftly. We have to get out of here!" Said Julie. As the three of them runs to the car of Angela's.

{Jessica make it at the store.   As people was taking pictures of
her horse.   The horse stands on two feet and start walking
around and land back on fours. The people was in
"shocked! Jessica grab a buggy and the people inside
stares   As she enter the store. { Jessica would
always believe sugar is poison for your body.'}
So she would pick out organic drinks and snacks. Even

chicken for her to bake. The Employee who was stacking
 can goods, would always
scratch his for-arm and yells at the shoppers. Jessica hear
the man, and act like she pay him no attention".
As it got worst, the man fall on his back and start sounding
like a sheep, and a goat. Shoppers was staring and some
called the police. When he open his eyes, he leap on his

CHAPTER : 11

on his feet and start running like a tiger and his mouth was open.
Shoppers start screaming and running. Some of the
men, try fighting him off and got bit. Jessica leaves her cart
and walks around the corner, to only see the man attacking
the men. Hey! Leave them alone. Said Jessica.
Who the hell are you? He asked. Im sending you out of
his body, and You dont belong here! Jessica said.
Suddenly, the man stands on two feet, and horns started
growing out of his body, and he leaps way into the
air and charge at Jessica. Jessica take out five pentagrams
and throw them at the same time and they enter
his body and he fall to the floor, shaking and he spoke
 tongues which nobody can under-stand. Accept Jessica.

I understand the words you speak! Jessica said As she get
on her knee and push the pentagrams inside his body. Dont

move!! shouted the voice, coming from behind. Im not the bad
person here". Jessica said. "she's trying to kill me!
Cried the man, who was laying on the floor. Jessica was arm-rested
and nobody said anything.

{Mean-while, Omen and Pitts returned back to the under-ground.
Omen start throwing things around. What happened?
Kacey asked. We was over powered by this woman! Said Omen.
That's crazy! Said Kacey. she's not normal. Pitts said.
Me and kacey will kill her! Said Tim. "What make you both
better than me? Omen asked. "Because, you cant do your
job right! Said Tim. As he stand face to face with Tim.

the blood will do the job. Said Pitts. we created so many
already! Omen said. "Always have a plan to make an
army. Said Pitts. As he stand by the pool of blood. What are

you creating now? Omen asked. Zombies and warlocks with
big nose and lots of weapons". Said Pitts.   As he cut
the center of his hand and holds it over the blood.
{the blood boiled, As Pitts kept his hand above the blood.
Suddenly, zombies with wide mouths, and teeth made out of horns,
approach out of the pool of blood.

Next, the warlock's approaches out of the pool of blood and
holding long knives that was pointy at the end.
The zombies show their teeth to the warlock's. you'll all

be working together!   Said Pitts. We want flesh and brains!
Shouted the zombies. We want the same too.! Said the
warlocks. "You all will be eating the sane thing! Said Pitts.

what did you summmond us to do? Asked one of the zombies.
Take your army and attack the innocent and
good! Said Pitts. What about us? One of the
warlocks asked. Your job is to feed off human fear
and emotion's. Said Pitts.   As the blood portal appear.
"Walk through that portal, and you'll be at your destination.

Said Omen. The warlocks shove the zombies out the way and
enters the blood portal. "Whats next for me? Kacey asked.
I want you to kill Joana. Said Pitts. Kacey smiles and enter

Julie, Angela and Zack drove for 3hr's until they run out of gas.
That sucks! Said Julie. "Maybe theres a gas-station ahead.
Angela said. "We all can walk. Said Zack. Will someone
break into the car? Julie asked. This car will take care of it
self." Zack Replied. As he get out of the car and so did Angela and

Julie. "A car is a thing". Angela said. "Lets keep walking, and watch your surroundings. Said Zack.   Look, Theres a farm! Shouted Julie. As she pointed. "Somebody will give us gas". Said Angela.   {Kacey made it at the hospital, as Joana was putting her stuff into her car.   Kacey pull out a knife and Joana "kick her down. What do you want with me? Joana asked. As the knife fall' out of Kaceys hand. Dont kill me, Pitts sent me to kill you!

Said Kacey.   You have a choice.! Joana said. Kacey hand move a-little, and a big white hand smash Kacey into pieces. swift'ly, Joana jump in the car and drives off. Kaceys body melt back to Pastor Pitts. "I told her she wasnt strong enough! Said Omen. She'll pay! Said Tim. As he stands over the pool of blood. Not to worry. Said Pitts.

CHAPTER : 12

{The old farm was covered in dust. As the windows was fogged up-
The roof - gave in and a pile of dead horses, laying around.
Who-ever did this, should be a-shame of themselves! Said Julie.
As The farm door was open. Me and Zack will check it
out and you keep watch! Said Angela. As her and Zack
enters the farm. Once they get inside, the farm was filled with tools
and bikes. Someone up there? Asked the voice of an old woman.
Zack and Angela search around until they see a trap-door.
Is somebody down there? Zack asked.
Im down here". The old lady Replied. Angela and Zack open
the Trap-door at the same time, and runs down the old dusty
steps. When they make it down-stairs, there was nothing but
darkness. "Nice for you both to join in"., said an old creepy
voice. As a light pop on and an old woman about 90, sitting in

a rocking chair, and her hair was long and dusty grey. How long you' been down here?? Angela asked.   200 years!   She said. As she was sitting in a silver wheel-chair.   We need to get you out of here. Said Zack.   "This place is already cursed!

she said. As the farm start shaking and her hair start to fall
out. As her face sink in and she stands out of the chair.
Long horns grow out of her head and reach the ground floor.
You should never had come here!! she shouted. Zack draw
his shot-gun and shoot at her. Bullets   dont kill me!

She said. Grabbing a large axe and Angela and Zack runs up-
stairs.   As Julie kept watch, a giant hole open
up and out come Zombies. We have trouble!!! Julie
shouted. Angela and Zack come running out of the farm, and grabs
Julie. What's going on? Julie asked.   Keep running!
Said Angela. As the three of them run down the road.

CHAPTER : 13

Powers was given to Lee and Heather. As Heather has pink wings
and Lee has golden wings. you're the highest of all!"
"Nothing immortal can kill the both of you! Said Cindy.
Thank you! Said Heather. As her and Lee touch the light pole
and vanish. Where are we now?   Heather asked. Look
like we;re in New-york". Said Lee. As he saw a Bar.
Im getting hungry! Said Heather.
let's go inside. Said Lee. a few women and men
check   Heather out. As they both enter the Bar. " You two new
in town? Asked the Bartender. "Yeah, do yo have any special

meals?   Lee asked. "Only hot-dogs and fries! The Bartender said.

a woman enter into the bar and askes for a
strong drink. Look, you gonna have to pay me this time!
He said. She reach in her pocket and slam the money on the
bar.. and look at Lee. "You from around here? She asked.

—

"you mean from another world? Lee asked. Yes! She said. putting
her chin down and smiling. "Here you two go". Said the
Bartender. Looks good! She said . You must be very creative?
Lee asked.   As she has spike hair and wear's a spike collar
and black make-up. and plus out-going clothing that was sexy."
That I am! how'd you know? She asked. Because you
dress different from everybody else and I like women who's
different!" Said Lee.   What's your name? She asked.

Clark ken! Said Lee. "That is such a lie! She said. "Keep it
down! I dont want anyone to notice me! Said Lee.
As he turn away and start eating. You didnt tell me your
name yet! She said. Malisa, is that you?? Heather asked.
"I didnt know you was sitting over there! Malisa said.
As she get up and hugs Heather. "Its been years, dude! Heather

Said.
{Jessica was taken to the station for question's. As Paul's The owner
of The department and was searching for Jessica since.
"Nice to see your pretty face again! Said Paul. You have nothing
on me". Said Jessica. You was trying to kill another person!!!
Shouted Paul. As he was walking around her, holding a bat.
Untie me! She { demands} him. Not this time,
you're about to get burn alive! Paul Shouted. As he leave from
her sight And close the door behind him. I need to get out of here".
Jessica "think'" to her'self. Suddenly, a sound of someone
chopping wood, approach her ears. "Rope of ashes. Said
Jessica and the rope change into ashes and rub off her arms.

{Heather and Malisa was playing pool and chatting, While Lee
eat' his food. A Shadow figure known as the Shadow man,
appear out-side the Bar holding a suit-case. All of a sudden..
he change

day into night. The suit-case open'
and out come elderly shadow women hunch over like a
creature haunting for food.   What the heck is that? Asked a
man with a long brown beard. It's The Shadow man.
 Malisa said. What do he want?! Heather asked.
.soul's. Malisa replied.   Dont open the door!!
shouted Heather. The man with the long brown beard and
three other guys run out-side and they was "attack."
I cant let my boys die! Shouted the Bartender. As he grab his
shot-gun from under the bar and four other guys went with

him. You hurt my friends, you gotta hurt me!! he shouted.
As he start shooting and the shadow man release more of
the elderly women who was fat and vanish into dark'ness.

suddenly, Black smoke spread inside the Bar. Up-stairs,
Hurry! Shouted Lee. As Heather and Malisa runs ahead of
him and up the stairs. Lee follow behind.   As The smoke
rise's. Too high to jump!   Said   Malisa. As she back

CHAPTER : 14

s away from the window. Lee found a rope and tie it around
a wooden bed. Get moving! Shouted Lee. Heather jumps out
the window and land on her feet while Lee and Malisa climb
down the rope.   when Malisa made it to the bottom she askes Heather,
How did you do that?? " Lucky jump!   Heather Said . There they
are! Shouted one of the elderly shadows. Keep running. Said Lee.

{In between times, Joana speeds on a-lonely silent road
because she wanted to get away from the scene.   She still couldnt
get over, why would that strange woman wanted to kill her.
All of a sudden, Joana nod off, and she pull over to the curb
and fall's-asleep.   Swiftly, a   light flash and the car with Joana
inside, vanish. The door open and Joanas body was remove from
the car and onto a white table. Joana open her eyes to only

see three colorful Aliens, with human feature's. Joana jump
off the table and looks around for a weapon.   What are
you creatures? Joana Asked. people call us aliens! One of
them Said. Pulling an I.V out of its arm and try to

approach her. Suddenly, Joana spins around and a man Appear,
holding a hammer. Theres no such thing as good Aliens.
 Said Joana. The man licks his hammer
and attack the three Aliens. After the job was done,
Joana look out the space-ship window and realize, she's no-longer
on Earth. Where was they taking you in the first place?
He asked Joana. I dont know. Joana said.

Jessica   sneak out of The Department and start running. As
Paul did'nt notice she escaped. As him and a few guys
was making a stake. The Department was no-longer
in her sight. As she run further and further. Suddenly,
she saw a brick house that was surrounded by apple
trees And decided to take shelter. "Can I

help you? Asked the voice of an older woman. "Im looking for
some-where to stay because my house's too far! Said Jessica.
As she put on a deguise of a help'less woman.

94

you poor child! She said.
The old lady wear's a black dress and about
6f2 and her hair was up. Why do you hold a gun in your
hand? Jessica asked. You cant be too friendly". She said
to Jessica. If I invaded your home, I should get on my way.
Come in". she said. Jessica smiles and enter the house.

{The ship was going into a black hole, But the man with the
hammer, turns the ship around. Five more Aliens enter the
ship. You didnt think we was gonna let you return to
earth, did you? One of them asked.
Keep driving the ship. I'll fix them! He said. As he approach
them with two hammers.   Now, which one of you space
demons wants to die!! he shouted.   Suddenly, The five of
them attack. The man with the Hammer spin around
and knocks them all down. Next, he smash   all of their
heads in. as blood was all over the floor. This is our ship!!
he shouted. "I see Earth from here! Said Joana. Great! He replied.
"For now, you're my body guard. Joana said. Hammer Law,
at your service! Said Law. All of a sudden, the Ship shut-
down. What now?? Joana asked.

they're trying to suck us in. said Law. Space is filled with gas.
Joana said. I have to find me a suit. Law said.
Joana open her arms and a helmet appear.. Good thinking!
Said Law. As he put on the Helmet and walk towards the
 exit. You ready? Law asked. Yes! Joana said and
she push the red button and out Law went Flying with two
hammers. As the botton of the Hammers – change into rockets. Coming!!
He shouted. As he land onto the wind-shield of the space ship.

Out of no-where, an Alien comes dressing in a karate uniform
and holding a golden spear in its hands.
you're not gonna take Joana from us! Said the Alien. As it
start attacking Law. Law block with his two Hammers

and trip the Alien on its back and try smashing its face.
the Alien kick one of the Hammers out of Law
hands and kick Law down and flip on its feet.
Next, the Alien pile-drive Law in his back and
put him in a head lock.   Come on Law, You can do this!
Said Joana. As the ship tilt left to right. Swiftly, Law
flip the Alien over and smash its head with the Hammer and
kick its body off the ship. Look like your boy wasnt
so tough after all! Said Law. As he smash the front ship
 and it start smoking. The Aliens in the ship try recovering
and Law smash the window and jump   off the ship. Ka-boom!!

CHAPTER : 15

after the ship was destroy, Law fly back into the ship.
Lets go home!   He said. As he sit down and smiles.
{Jessica exam the Ravens. Arent
they cute? She asked Jessica. "So rare for some'one to
keep Ravens as pets! Jessica said. I grew up with ravens, when I
was a little girl! "Thats why they call me Ravia". She said.

Very Charming! Said Jessica. Suddenly, the phone ring.
It must be my son." "I'll be right back!   Said Ravia.
Leaving Jessicas sight. Ravia swiftly answer the phone,
by holding it up to her left ear. Hello? Ravia answers.   Im look
ing for a woman name Jessica! Paul Said.   "Shes at my
house. "{ Whisper} Ravia. Keep her company until I get   there.
Said Paul. Ravia hang up the phone and walk back into
the living room. That cop is your son? Jessica asked.
Swiftly, Ravia turn into a Raven mixed with a beast face.
You aint going no-where!!! Ravia shouted. As her feet was
made of Raven'   and she use them to attack Jessica.

Jessica's hair light up white and green, and she back kick Ravia
through the house and runs out of the front door. Going somewhere?
Paul asked. Pointing a gun at her. Suddenly, strong wind
blow and horse shoes approach from out of nowhere
and run Paul over. You found me! Jessica said. As she climb
on the horse and fly' away. {Joana and Law made it back
to earth and Julie, Zack, and Angela stood back from the
ship. As the door was let down and out come Joana and Law.
Dont shoot, we're humans! Said Law. How did you get a
ship? Julie asked. Its a long story! Joana said. As her
and Law approach the three of them. My name's Joana and
this's Hammer Law. Said Joana.   These are my friends!
Angela, and Zack And im Julie". Julie said.
Seems like you'll be needing Team work to kill us all".
Said The orange moon." you're the one who started
this blood for power crap! Said Julie. Do you think
by going to the light side will save your soul?" The orange moon
asked. I was never meant to be a moon! Said Julie. And that's why
Death is freedom! The Orange Moon said.

Suddenly, Law throw his hammer at Orange. "You cant hit me
silly man! As the Hammer reverse and hit Law in the head.

100

CHAPTER : 16

now, the last battle is about to begin. Said   orange moon. How do you
mean? Angela asked. The moon start puking
blood every-where and the sky becomes blood red and everything
start changing around them. So did the world where Lee
and Heather was.   Master? Orange has started the battle.
I'll relocate   somewhere else and you moons kill all   of them.
Said Pitts.   The moons enter the blood portal and vanish.
"Nice for you all to visit!   Said Lee. As he Join   with
Julie, Gabe and the rest of the white-kingdom army.

This is a beautiful place!   sky painted with
blood."   everything painted all red, "Just like
the ones that crossed us was killed.   we're gonna kill
you all next.! Said Omen.   You shall pay for their lives! Shouted Julie.
Taking   their lives felt very joyable ! Said Tim. Attack!!!!!
shouted Omen.   The moons and all   of The evil   creatures,
charge   at   Lee and his army. Angela start shooting and
Gabe swings   his cane around and knock some of the zombies
down. The shadow man grab Jessica by her neck and try
to get inside her mouth. Swiftly, law strike'" the shadow man
from behind.   Thanks! Said Jessica . As she get on the Horse

and fly over the army of zombies. Causing them to fight their
own kind.   You little witch!! Shouted Orange. As he try puking
blood on her. Jessica dodge' to the right and   charge at the moon.
you're too early! Said the moon. As it blow Jessica to the
ground. Before Julie run to check on Jessica, Omen put

Julie in a head-lock and throw her to the ground. Thought you
learned your lesson, when we almost beat you to death!
Said Omen. Suddenly, Omen's head was cut off by the
sword of Leeporder. Tim become shock. As his eyes grew
large. "Need a hand? Lee asked. Thank you! Said Julie.
As she was being helped up. Swiftly, Tim tackle Lee to
the ground and Julie kick him in the face. Tim kicks
Julie to the ground and Lee punch Tim 5 x in the face
and cut' off his head. Seem like we're winning! Said
Gabe. Suddenly, loud horns blow and out of the blood comes
white-knights, riding on horses along-side with warriors.

Charge!!! shouted Cindy. So, we meet again! Said Ravia. As she

grab Jessica by the hair and the horse open its mouth and swollow
her.   Lee confront the orange moon.   Its just you and me!
Said Lee.   Are you kidding me! Said the orange moon. As
it grows   two arm's and two leg's and start attacking Lee.
Lee block with his evo and legs.   As they watch from
below.   Swiftly, Lee   punch the moon in the eyes and
 blood pours out.   My wonderful eyes!!! it cries!

Suddenly, Lee fly   a few feet away and his whole body powers

up. grab hold to each-other! This is gonna be a powerful   punch.
Said Lee. Swiftly, the moon charge at Lee in full
speed, Trying to kill him with the foot of death. Lee
punch the moon and everything explode'.
When Angela and the rest uncovers their eyes, everything
was back to normal.   A truck stop in the middle of the
road. You guys alright?   Asked an older man who was
dressed in blue-jeans and a farmer brown shirt. Yes. Angela

Replied.   We taking a rest here because we are on our way to
vegas. Said Julie.   Thats where im from! He said.
Can you give us a lift?   Angela asked.   Sure thing, officer!
{So there-fore, the man get into the truck and Angela,
Julie and Heather jumps into the back and off the man drives
into the distance. Leaving everything behind. As they all look back.}

"DONT TURN THE PAGE YET"

{now that was close". I can assure you thought this was the ending
of this fiction, fantasy story". there's no need to throw
your sock's off, my dear readers.
What happen next? you'll ask. I can not tell you". What
I can tell you is… their Journey dont stop here".
By turning to the next page, will take you to another Journey,
leaving you in chills, passion and Emotions.
So sit back, and enjoy the excitemet im about to give you readers".
Truly yours! You may start the next Journey please!"

107

CHAPTER :   17

Michelle is a beautiful english woman who dream of seeing other
worlds and talking to birds because the birds helps her
to be free and to see clearly out of the boring rich life.
And of course, a complex relationship. She also wears
dresses that match her eyes. you been in that window,
far too long! Said her mother. As she has long black
hair and wears a black dress and carrys a sword with
her. { Everyone calls her, miss Mocking way.}

Dont you ever knock? Michelle asked. Your husband james is down
stairs! Her mother said. Tell him I want some time to my'
self! Dont make me send the guards!! Mocking said in a
impatient tone. Michelle leave the window and exit her
room.   Mocking lock the window and exit the room. Why
did you keep me waiting? James asked. She was talking to
the birds. Mocking said. Are you crazy or something?
James asked. As he fix his glasses and his red tie and
cow-boy hat. Show some respect to the woman you love!
Said Michelle. Dont speak that way to him! Mocking Said.
I wish for you to stay out my relationship, mother! Michelle

said.   As she leave out the door with james. So they arrive at
the Bar. Michelle only gets out to see Englands
most famous bar. Im no bar woman! Said Michelle.
Just get inside! Said James. As he grab her arm and they
both enters the bar.   You didnt tell me you had a girl-friend!
Said his friend Bash.   Is that so?   Asked. Michelle.

Go and have fun! Said James. As he leave her sight.
Michelle becomes cold inside and she left the Bar and start
walking home. {Since then, Pitts was the only one left alive.
As he made his way to Englands under-ground.
Very nice place to create more evil! Said Pitts. As he stands
near the tub of blood.   Thats it! I'll create hockey demons.
Pitts said. As he come up with an idea of his own.
So he created Hockey sticks and throw them into
the blood. Hockey of deaths, come out my friends and be
born again!! Shouted. Pitts. The blood spill over and out come
twenty Hockey demons in uniforms.   You all look amazing!

said Pitts. The Hockey demons bows to pitts in a
approaching manner. you're too kind, Get up!
Pitts said. at your service. Said the lead Hockey
member. I want you to kill every innocent person in
England. Said Pitts. Suddenly, the Demons puts their sticks
together and vanish. Now, there's one more to create". Said Pitts.

so michelle made it at back home, and she stumbles towards the kitchen.
Are you mad, wheres James?? asked the guard who wears
a black suit.   I can take care of my'self! Michelle said. As she
grab her a drink and sit at the table. Who is it at
this moment? Asked Mocking. He was at the bar! Michelle
said. Its his wish for you to be there! Mocking said.
I despite his wishes and accept my own.! Michelle replied.
You wouldnt be rich if it wasnt for him!   Mocking shouted!
Money dont move me! Only freedom does! Michelle said.

James was sitting at the bar chatting with few women, until…
Bash tell him. that his wife had left.
James   leave   the   bar.   {The   Hockey   Demons   appears
from   the   under- ground   and   start skating into the
city.   Three   band   members   was   drinking under
the   bridge until one of the hockey Demon's kill each one of
them with a puck, with spikes on it. The   demons laugh
and drink's what-ever was left.   Whats our next move?

Asked one of the Demon's . We stay here until night,
so human's cant see us in the day. Said the demon who's
name Puck spike.   James "crash" through the front
door.   Where are you Michelle? He called.   she's washing
clothes. Mocking said. Standing by the basement door.
James run down the stairs to confront Michelle.   you
could of been killed!!! He shouted.   Why do you raise your
voice? Michelle asked.   Because, you know how dangerous
it is out there! James shouted. "I rather die to become free".
Michelle said.   Stop with all of this mad talk! James shouted.

Michelle put the clothes into the dryer and try walking away.
James grab her and start kissing her. She look away.
As she hug him. at night, Mocking was having a

114

CHAPTER : 18

birth-day party.   As Michelle sit on the
stairs, drinking red wine.   Care for a dance? James asked.
Im fine alone! Said Michelle. Im starting to dislike you!
James said. "You dont want him angry at you! Said Bash.
As he was dressed in a jump suit and has orange hair
and combat boots on. {Michelle leaves them, to
join the party.}   She think she's above your command".
Said Bash. I can see that now! James said. As he rub
his hair and show his teeth, and drinks his wine. What's
going on? Mocking asked. she's starting to get out of
hand! Said James. "Most men put their wives in their place".
Said Mocking. Nice to meet you Michelle! one of
Mocking friends said. You must be Michelle?
asked Dolly. As her hair was up in braids. So Dolly,
How long have you and my mother been friends? Michelle

asked. Hi, im James and this is my wife Michell!. Said James.
Oh, nice to meet you James! Said Dolly. (Michelle couldn't
believe how rude he was. As she walks away to talk to other

men. Who' stands in the crowd of people.
Suddenly, one of them asked for a dance. I accept". Michelle
said. As   they go to dance. Bash whispers
in James ear. James look over and see Michelle dancing
with another man and becomes angry}}   The man was
very tall and has black hair.   "Whats your name? He asked.
"Can we just dance? Michelle asked. " Alright! he said.

James push the man and Michelle. Are you gone mad?
The man asked James.   The crowd of people stop and
stare.   Its my wife you're dancing with}}}   shouted James.
Suddenly, the man punch james in the face and bash and two other
guys carry him out of the House.
Everyone continues to enjoy the party. As   James
recover and look' for Michelle.   Michelle stands by the ocean
until bash approach her. Why are you giving him
a hard time? Bash asked.   I dont have to answer to you!

Michelle said. Suddenly, james push her down and she roll into the water. you'll answer to me! Michelle gets up and try to run. But James grab her by the hair. Let me go! She cried. How dare you dance with another man?!! James shouted. I wish I didnt marry you! Said Mitchelle. James slap her to the ground and start kicking her.

CHAPTER : 19

now, who's the boss? James asked. you're. Michelle said. As
blood pours out of her mouth. Come on James, you dont
want to kill her. Said Bash. As they walks away. Michelle
sit up, holding her stomach. How does the pain fill...?
Asked   the creepy voice, coming from the darkness. whos there?
Michelle asked. In a curious tone. Do you really want to
know?... swiftly, Michelle get up and run for her life.

as   foot steps approach out of the darkness.
The next, morning, Michelle opens her eyes and see bars on her
window. As the maid opens the curtain. Lisa, Whats going
on? Michelle asked.   Your mother said you're to be locked
in for five days. Lisa said. Im a grown woman. Michelle
said. jumping out of the bed to exit her room.

{Way on the north side of England lived Camron,
and she play for a Hockey team name { step up .}
 she's confident, and cocky and always wears
her hair up. As she was playing on ice, two of
her opponents try to ram her against the glass. But she evo
them. Causing them to fall down. Next, she hits the puck
into the net and everyone cheered. After the game,
the team celebrated at a pizza joint. Suddenly, Camrons
Iphone ring. Hello? Camron answers.   Im locked in
for five days! Said Michelle.   What do you mean??
Camron asked. Please come over! Michelle cried.
Stay there, I'll be over. Said Camron. As she get up from the
table and jump in the car .   Michelle had to wash the
dishes, While two guards   watch her. "No fun to be
watched! Said Mocking.   James unhanded me! Said Michelle.

And who fault is that? Mocking asked. So you're saying

121

its okay for him to beat your daughter?? asked Michelle.
should of took his kindness! Swiftly, Michelle throw a plate at
her mothers head and the two Guards grab Michelle and put
her in cuffs. throw her in the basement!! shouted Mocking.
Suddenly, the two guards throw her down the basement stairs.

nice of you to join in. said a body builder guard.
Michelle holds her side and get off the floor. Hey, I wont
hurt you! He said. Michelle picks up a paint bucket and
throw it at his head and run to the base-ment window.
No bars on it! She said to her -self. The guard shakes
it off and go after her. Michelle climb on an old
wooden table and try to climb out the window.
But he grabs her and throw her in a wooden chair, and then
grab a hammer from a tool box. Time to eat, Lex!!
Shouted Mocking. Lex hit one of her knees and walks away.

Michell takes the pain by squeezing the chair of the arm.
When the door closed, thats when she limp her way
to the base-ment window. She put one healed leg
on-top of the table and thats when the base-ment door open.
Im taking my lunch down   stairs. Said Lex.
Michelle pull' her-self onto the table and climb out the window.
She escape out the base-ment window!!!   shouted Lex.
Suddenly, a car pulls up and it was Camron.   where's
Michelle?   Camron asked. Shes gone missing! Mocking said..

CHAPTER : 20

The back door opens and Michelle climb inside. Drive me away".
Michelle said. Keep your head down.." said Camron.
I'll go search for her. Said Camron! Thank you dear! Said
Mocking and Camron drives off. Search by the ocean.
Said Mocking. As the guards search by the ocean, suddenly,
they was beeing attack by hockey sticks and Lex charge
at them and a skate was throw at his head and it was pull

out of his head and lex fall' on the ground. Was he value enough?
Asked Puck spike . As he rub her hair. no.! said Mocking.
"good! He said. Im looking for Michelle. Mocking   said.
Maybe we can work out a deal! Said Puck. As
a contract appear to her face.   Whats this
contract for?   Mocking Asked. Sign this contract, and you'll
become part of the crew".   Said Puck.

So, if I sign this contract, you'll work for me and I'll have
powers? Mocking asked.   "Indeed". it said . Deal! Said Mocking.

{black santics was created, and their job was to
put ashes in the eyes of the living.
black mary was also created to feast on souls, and to
trick love ones and the living.   Camron arrive to only see
a wingless man, laying in her drive-way.

Do you see what I see? Michelle asked. A man with wings!
Camron said. As she get out of the car with a knife in
her hand. Sir, Are you okay? Camron asked. The man
move a little. he's alive. Said Michelle. Maybe we should
call the police. Camron said. Thats a bad idea. He said.
As he struggles to get on his feet.   Who are you?!
Camron asked. My name's Leeporder and I come from a
different universe! Said Lee. "Im Michelle and this is my
best friend, Camron! Seem like you been abused!
Said Lee. I fell down some stairs!" Michelle said. Lying
only makes it worst". Said Lee. What do you mean
universe?   Asked Camron. "Wouldmt you like to know!

Playfully said Lee.   Are you a fallen Angel? Camron asked.
You read too many bibles! Lee said. Is everything alright
Camron? asked miss jones. Who live next door. " i won
the game! Said Camron. I knew you can do it! Said Jones.
As she was wearing a robe. Why is she wearing a
robe? Lee asked. She think she' a queen.! Said Camron.
Good night, miss Jones! Said Michelle. Whats that smell?
Camron asked. We must get inside! Said Lee. Camron
swiftly unlock the front door. As Lee and Michelle
runs in at the same time. Michelle lock the door behind her.
Turn the lamp off. Said Lee. As he run to the window.

You starting to scare me! Said Camron. Both of you, come here.
Said Lee. Michelle and Camron walk towards the window and
see' a woman standing in the middle of the
street, facing the moon. She's wearing a long black dress,
 with black blood
running down it. Next, she has wolf ears that was longer
than her head and her nails was shaped like claws.
What the heck is that? Camron asked.   Michelles heart start

beating fast. show no fear, Or it'll find you. Said Lee.
What do we do? Michelle asked. I have to confront her. Lee
said. Leaving them behind.   Black Marys
left ear open and she turn to confront Lee, As he approach her.
 Her face is mixed with a beast and a bat. Why are you

CHAPTER : 21

130

here? Lee asked. I want life, and yours too!
She said.   Suddenly, the phone rings in Camron's house.
Hello? Michelle answers.   Where are you? Im worried sick
about you! James said.   You just un-handed me!   Said Michelle.

Look, I was drunk that night and I feel horrible as a man!
James Replied. I dont know! Said Michelle. Im at your house,
Maybe we can talk   this out. Said James. { As Camron
was watching out of the window, Michelle slip way.
Black Mary try to choke Lee with her claws but
Lee breaks her arm with a single hand chop.
Michelle jump into the car and drives off.   What are you
doing??   asked Camron.
The lights turn on and the door open, and out comes
Miss Jone. Hmm," thats weird. Said Miss Jones . As she
Close the door and turn   the lights off. Lee continues
to battle Mary.   But Mary falls to her death, by

using the wings. Next, he look around to see if anyone in
sight and burn her body. All of a sudden,
black blood pours down the sewer drain. She took my car!!
Shouted Camron. I have to go save her. Said Lee. What if one

of those things come back? Camron asked.   What's your weapond?
Lee asked. My fist and Hockey stick! Camron said.
Hold out your hand. Said Lee. Camron hold out her hand
 and Lee writes two capital letters,   {W.K } and step backwards.
What it stand's for? Camron asked.   Its your powers!
Lee said. As he fly away into the sky. So Michelle arrive
at   the house. As James wait   for her on the porch.
When she exit the car, James run   off the porch
and hug her.   Where have you been??
He asked. As he Look   around. I have to take a long ride
out! Michelle said. James pull   her close and
 put her in a bear hug. You're hurting me!
Michelle said.   Drive the car into the ocean!!   shouted
Mocking. You lied to me!!!   shouted Michelle. As she
try struggling out of his bear hug. Lee fly   and

knocks them both down and then land. James swiftly pull out a gun and it was shot out of his hand. Your fast…! But not fast enough! Said Skippy. Who are you three? Mocking asked. How could you do this to your daughter? Lee asked. She had to learn her lesson! Said Mocking. As the Hockey demons appear out of darkness. { Camron got through packing her gear and left a message to her coach. From down stairs, the door close. Its me, Michelle! Said Michelle. Camron grab her gear and run down stairs. Where were you? Camron asked. Your car's in black blood. Michelle

Replied.   As her eyes spin in circles.   How's that?   You just
left!   Camron said.   Michelle put her head down.
Are you okay??   Camron asked.   Stop asking me silly questions!
As   the voice start changing.   Camron step away from
Michelle. As hooks grow out of her hands.
you're not my best-friend!
Said Camron. As she pull one of her hockey sticks out

134

strikes mary in her head and runs out the front door, and
down the street. {Mocking attacks Michelle. By trying to
put a knife in her chest. Suddenly, Skippy shoot her and
Michelle gets up. Run to the ocean! Said Lee.
Why? Asked Michelle. The ship is waiting for us. Said Lamar.

When Michelle turn to face the ocean, she
see' a big white ship and couldnt believe her eyes.
Its so beautiful! She said . Skippy grab Michelles hand
and start running to the ship. Lee knock all the
Hockey demons down and block their path with salt.
We will find you! One of the demons shouted Dont try it".
Lee said. As he start walking away. The ship sails off.
As they all make it A - board. I cant believe im leaving england!
Said Michelle. Wait for me! Shouted Camron. }

CHAPTER : 22

Mean while..
{ Angela, Julie and Heather was chatting on the back
of the truck until... all four tires blow out. Darn it!! shouted the
man . As he get out of the truck. What could of cause it?
Angela asked I dont know. These are new tires. He
said .   Look, Theres a big hotel over there! Said Julie.
It looks really spooky". Heather said. As it was covered in
dust and surrounded by dead grass and trees .
we'll go and check it out. Said Angela.   As her and the old
man leave their sight, to approach the hotel.

Julie and Heather sits back in the truck. I didnt catch your name,
sir! Angela said. My name's Bob the farmer! Said Bob.
Nice to meet you Bob! Angela said. Same to you officer!
Bob replied. When they get closer to the entrance of the Hotel,
the door opens by it'self. Leaving them both
in a total surprise". As silents approach
them from the inside. Angela draws her gun and enter
the building cautiously. Is anyone here? Angela asked.
As she saw' the chairs covered with white sheets-
and the front desk that sat by the entrance was still clean
and the carpet dusty.   someone's here said Bob.

As he wipe the desk with his finger. How can you
tell? Angela asked.   The desk is still clean! Bob said.
If I were you, I'll run out of this place. Said a woman
who peek from behind the desk. Her hair's colored in
dark pink and she wears glasses and about a heavy set woman.

we're not looking to get booked. Our truck tires blew out and
we're looking for help. Angela said. Let me call eat – em!
She said. Angela look to see,' that the wall's
changed red. Wasn't these walls white at first? Bob
asked These walls does that because its fading out. She
said . Hanging up the phone. So, whats your name and
how long have you been working here? Angela asked.
My name is Kelly and I been working here for years! Kelly said.
Do you have a rest-room? Bob asked. Its right around the
corner. Kelly said. As she cough in her hand and
look around. Bob enter the hall on the right and
becomes dizzy
 and fall on his knees and that's when he see a bull
mix with a horse head and male body . Bob couldnt
believe his eyes. As he reach for the rest-room' door
and everything become normal again. When Julie and Heather
was sleeping, an old tow-truck, pull up.

out of the tow-truck, comes a creepy old man and his hair's
short grey
and skin sunken in and wear's a mechanic uniform.
 Suddenly, he spit and knocks on the window.
Julie rolls down the window to greet the man. Its gonna
cost you! Said eat'em. Im sorry, he's inside the hotel!
Julie said. The man turn away and start walking to
the hotel.   That guy look like he came out of Jail!
Heather said.   I agree, But as long as he can fix the truck!"
Said Julie.

{Black mary breathe new life into Mocking.
Im alive again! Said Mocking. As she felt her body
and her face.   Your daughter shall die and the ones with her!
Said Black Mary. We cant let them get away with this!!
James shouted.   holding a shot-gun.
Look like they're long gone! Said Mocking. As she stand' by the ocean.
Out of the ocean, appear a ship with 200 battle

140

CHAPTER : 23

Cannons and the ship was covered in black blood. Black santa
clauses on ships?? Jame's asked. Come aboard!!
One of the Santic's shouted! Lets get going. Said Black
Mary. As she walk ahead of them, dragging her dress.

{Camron made it on-board. As they sailed further into the
north. The wind and ocean was very calm
and Michelle looks over board of the ship. You okay?
Asked Lee. I want to thank you for breaking me out of
that awful life! She said. How do you feel at this
moment? Lee asked Michelle look away into the distance
 and the wind blow' through her hair. I feel free!
She said. Lee put' his hand on her shoulder, and walk away into
the distance. She stares at him, until he was out of her sight.
You like him huh? Camron asked. Way better than James!
She said. Why did you drive off like that? Camron
asked. I thought he was a change person, but he's
still the same! Said Michelle. Never go back to a
man who keep abusing you. Camron. Said. As she hug

Michelle and stares off into the distance with her. When Lee
approach the wheel deck, there he see a giant sea creature,
go back under water. Did you see that?   Skippy asked.
I saw it. Be on alert.! Lee said. Swiftly, the ship
rock' from left to right.   Michelle
and Camron falls down.   Out of the ocean appear, a

giant goat mixed with a fish body and it start attacking the ship.
Michelle become' scared. As she runs away.   This is
not your ship! Shouted Camron! Lamar run and set off
the cannons But the goat creature dodge to the left.
Causing the cannons to miss. Next, it bite on the ship
and Camron   strikes it in the eyes, with her Hockey stick
and it went back into the ocean. Camron smiles and put
up her middle finger.   Swiftly, two goat creatures
comes rising out of the ocean and they fought over who
was gonna attack first.   Lee spread his wings and fly
to the creature's and punch both of their eyes out.
Both sea creatures try to bite Lee and Skippy and
Lamar shoot them in the neck and Lee pull   out a
long sword and cut their

heads off.   The sea creatures vanish by turning into black
blood and it sink   back into the ocean and back into
Pitts hand.   he's stronger than I thought! Said Pitts. As

CHAPTER : 24

you killed the english sea creature, that everyone was talking about!
Said Michelle.   Full speed a-head! Shouted Lee. Skippy
pulls the gear   and the ship went forward in
full speed and everyone falls down.   {The man eat'em,
greeted Angela and asked for an up-front pay. Angela then
tells him she's not the owner and he decided to do it for
free. Bob approach with a weird look on his face. what's
wrong? Angela asked.   On my way to the rest-room, I
just saw the weird'est thing! What thing? Kelly asked.

Its hard to remember". Bob said. Would you like a glass of
water? Kelly asked.   Sure. Said Bob. Kelly leaves his sight.
As she goes to fetch him a glass of water.   When my truck
get fixed, we need to get out of here! Said Bob.
As Kelly enter the kitchen, the creature was standing by the
sink. As it was chewing on its teeth and nails.   Dont worry,
lunch will be ready soon! Kelly said. How long will it
take? The creature asked. When the Hotel slowly sink.
Kelly said. As she fill the glass with water and leave its sight.

Julie and Heather stands out-side the truck. As eat-em walk to his
tow-truck to grab four tires. I miss Lee! Said Julie.
He destroyed the moon and vanish! Heather said. Staring off
into the distance. You like him to dont you?" Julie asked. Look,
its just a battle thing! Heather said. As she look at eat-em
and he was holding a saw in his hand. Heather pull Julie aside.

Whats you problem? He asked. As he saw the tire off
and jack the truck up. Kelly looks at Angela and Bob and
her hair start falling out. Whats wrong with my hair?   she asked.

Angela and Bob puts on the most desturbing look on their face ".
as it got worse and the doors closes. It's starting to get
hot! Said Bob. As the wall's and furniture
start melting. Angela jumps back. As Kells whole skin
burn off and she was a pig-devil. We need to get out of
here! Shouted Angela. As she run towards the stairs and it
was melting also. Left side of the hall! Shouted Angela.

as her and Bob runs through the hall. there's no escaping!
Kelly said. As she jump over the desk and runs after them.
 Look, The Hotel is sinking!   Shouted Julie".   Dont move!
Eat'em shouted. As he grabs Julie from behind and press the
sharp of the saw against her neck.   Why are you doing this?
Heather asked.   You people should have not come here!
He said. As the Hotel was sinking further into the ground.
Look, we just want the truck fixed. Heather said.   Get in the
tow-truck! He shouted. Heather walks towards the Tow-truck.
holding up her hands.   No funny stuff or I'll cut
her throat! He said. When Heather made it to the truck,
she open the door and gets inside.   You kinda smell good!
He said.   As he start smelling her hair and push her to walk
towards the Hotel.   What are you doing? Julie asked. I want
to intoduce you to my home! Eat'em replied.   But its too
hot down there! Said Julie. Suddenly, two of her arrows shoots
out of her pouch and shoot straight into his eyes.   Julie
kick him straight through the entrance door and run   inside.

find them, I'll stop the Hotel from sinking down. Said Heather.
Julie smiles and runs inside. Leaving Heather behind.
Angela and Bob comes to a dead-end. As she take's off her
jacket and throw it to the ground. Look like the tempature
went up! Said Kelly. As she slowly walks towards
them. Angela start " shooting. But Kelly kept
walking. As the gun bullets sink into her skin.

Before Kelly take another step, five arrows was shot into her
head and Kelly start burning all over. The sound
of a pig squeal". As she vanish. Julie?"
cried Angela. Suddenly, the creature rush out of nowhere
and grabs Bob by his neck and open its mouth . Help!.. Help!...
He shouted. Angela runs to pull Bob by his legs. But the
creature was too strong. Julie shoot five arrows in its
mouth and it let go. As the inside of its mouth begin to swell.
Lets get out of here! Shouted Julie. As the walls and
floors start opening and hands reaching out to grab the
three of them. Hurry up! Shouted Heather. As she was
still holding the Hotel. Suddenly, the three of them
jumps out of the Hotel and land on the grass and
Heather release the Hotel . Bob still was in shocked" .

150

CHAPTER ; 25

We need to keep moving. Said Angela. As she help
Bob on his feet. { The pub's are filled with people and also
covered by night as-well. As it sat by the ocean".
Saoirse Dublin
is a warrior princess of ireland because her father fought
with the iron age who won the war against the british army.

Your father fought brave'ly. Said Findley tips. As he pours her
another drink. Saoirse is a confident, passion woman, who
loves adventures and mystic battles. Including going out-doors.
Her hair is long and dark orange and she always wears it in a
french braid that runs down to her lower back.
she's also wearing a green blouse, matching her pants and boots.
As two iron guns clips onto her waist buckle.
her face is round and smooth and has the look that'll make
any man fall in love with her".   Her brother name is Drew
Dublin and he's 18 years old and more of a beta male type.
he has short orange hair like his sister and only carrys a knife.
Unlike sairose, he only wear's normal clothing such as brown
pants and a white t-shirt that came with his green jacket.

where's my money Drew? Asked Tom. As he push Drew
against the building. Trying to escape us? One of his friends
asked. Look, I dont have any money! Drew said. One
of Toms friends go into his pocket and pull out a knife.

Please Tom, I'll get you your money the next day! Drew said.
Your brothers in trouble! One of the pubs shouted. Saoirse
jump from the bar and run out -side to only see her brother
getting slap". Leave him alone! Saoirse shouted. Pointing
the gun at them. Lets go! Tom said. As him and his friends

runs away. Thank you! Said Drew. What are you doing down
here? Saoirse asked. Uncle Robert wants you to come
home. Said Tom. Im a grown woman and I dont need his
permission! Saoirse said. Come home, Saoirse!
Said Robert. As he's big and has a long orange beard. How did
you get down here? Drew asked. How do you mean?

Saoirse asked.   He was drinking beer and watching tv!.. Drew said.

get home, Drew! Said Robert. As his beard turns black.
Run towards me! Said Saoirse. Drew look at
Robert and start walking away.   she's not your uncle, I am!!!

Robert shouted. Suddenly, a ship crash into the dock and Robert
vanish. "Have you ever heard of breaks? Lamar asked.   The
boat dont have breaks! Skippy said. Its call a
ship! Michelle said.   They both look the same to me! Said
Skippy. As he performs a front flip off the ship and land
on his feet. Who are they? Drew asked.   I dont know.
We must'nt trust them. Saoirse said. As she had both
hands on her guns, ready to shoot. Look like Dublin!
Said Michelle. As she unboard the ship and looks around.
Its so silent! Said Camron.   You need to leave, we're not
looking for trouble! Shouted Drew.   "we're Adventures!

said Lamar. As he put up his hands.

they seem alright! Said Saoirse. As she remove her hands from
her guns. Welcome to Ireland! Said Drew. As he go
to approach them all.   Saoirse look at Lee and walk
back into the pub. So, how did it go? Find asked.
They took off running. Saoirse said. Drinking up her
beer.   Lee and the rest of the crew, enters   the
pub. This place is sick! Said Camron. As she walk
towards the games and Michelle sit at the bar. You guys
seem different". Said Find. " Adventures.! Said Lamar.

Black mary dock the ship.   As The Hockey demons jump off
board and hide into The shadow of the night.
 As a few people exit the Pub to start chatting.
From the darkness, three Hockey pucks strike the three
of them in the head and their bodies was drag away. Next, the
power go out.   What the heck?!   Find. Said.
As he walk from behind the bar to look out the window.

the rest of the pub lights are out!   Said Find.   They' must
of   followed us.   Said Skippy.   Who?   Asked Drew.
Do you know how to shoot a gun?   Lamar asked.   I know
how to use a knife!   Drew   said. As his eyes was filled
with fear. he's never used a gun in his life. Said Saoirse.
 geting up from the bar to look   out the window.
Why are those people standing
out there?   Lee asked.   As he run   out of the pub to warn
them.   Get back inside! Said Lee.   For what?   Asked
a fat irish lady.   Something paranormal is here!   Lee   said.

The people of the pub, turn's their back to Lee and kept chatting.
Before Lee enter back into the pub,   the sound of ice
skating, approach out of The night and it was the Hockey
demons.   Lee toss a trash can at the demons and run   back
inside.   What are those creature's??   Find asked.
Suddenly, an ice skate was throw through the window and
hit Finds   in the head.   O-mg!!   shouted Drew. As he run
and hide' under the pool table.   Lamar and Skippy   start
shooting at the Hockey demons and some of them turn
into white smoke.   Can normal bullets kill them? Saoirse
asked.   " Only bullets that's paranormal. Lee   said. Thats different!

159

Saoirse said.
{In between time, Bob, Angela, and Julie was no-longer insight
of The hell's hotel. And not even close to Las vegas.
Bob was speeding so fast, he turn down the wrong road
that lead them into a ghost town. where are
we? Heather asked. Look like a town that use to
have value! He joke'ly said. Suddenly, the truck
cuts off and Bob try starting it. Out of gas! Bob
shouted. This is the wrong place to happen at. Angela
said. As she cock" her gun. Julie looks out the window. As
wind and silents was the only thing in sight. Bob gets out of
the truck to grab a gas can out the back .
 What are you doing? Julie asked. Getting gas!
Bob said. Its too dangerous! Heather said. Thinking it was a crazy idea.

I can take care of my'self!" Said Bob. As he pull out a hand
gun and shows it to them and walk away into the distance.
{a mystic alley that was hidden from their eyes, send out
a group of men, chatting and laughing".
Well… well… " said an african man wearing braids
and dirty clothes on. The two man was dressed the same
but only caucasian. Dont move! Angela said. Three of
the men stop and put their hands up. "We mean no harm, officer!
One of them said. Go back where you came from. Said Julie.

CHAPTER : 26

161

The two men step inside the African mans body, and
transform into a black cow and half-man.   Heather tap' her head
and the cow was still there. Impossible! Angela said.

{After the war was over. Jessica only arrive to see
her home on fire. Get out of here!! shouted the neighborhood.
I was only trying to save that man". Said Jessica.
With an innocent look on her face.
The Neighborhood refuse to hear and start throwing
rocks at her. Jessica rides away
into the distance.   By leaving the past behind her.
Jessica makes a quick stop at the Thrift shop and enter the
building. Next, she dressed in goth pants amd a tank top.
while
People take pictures of her horse. Swiftly, Jessica exit
the building and mounted her Horse and fly back
 on her journey again.   {The black cow man start throwing
cans at Julie, Heather and Angela.   You three woman aren't
strong enough for me!   Said the black cow man.   Angela
shoot' the cow man in the   stomach and   start pouring blood.

he looks at his stomach and start charging at them.
Bob found a gas-station that was 2 miles from the truck.
As The gas station seem empty.
So he thought nothing of it and decided to enter The gas
station. Behind the counter worked a fat man

with dark skin and he's wearing a mechanic uniform.
 What do you need?!
He asked Bob in a mean tone. I need some gas, please!
Said Bob. As he open his wallet
and put   10$ on the counter. Pump 6! said the man.
As he watch Bob exit the station and walk toward's   pump
6. clap!" clap!"   as he signal The four men to go
running   out of The gas-station to rob Bob.
While Bob fill   the gas can, The   four men approaches   him.

Can I help you gentle-men?   Bob asked.   We want your money!
One of the men said. As he's wears
a clown mask and the other holding a pipe, and   the third
has demon claws. Look, I dont have any money.
I   spent it on gas. Said Bob. Last chance. Said the man.
As the other grip his pipe. Suddenly, the sound of a truck
was being flip over and Bob make' a run for it.
Swiftly, the man with the demon claws jump over
Bob and dig his claws into his head and Bob become

a demon as well and the men take his money and walks away.
Heather ride the cow mans back, punching him in the
head. While The cow-man fight and attack Julie and Angela.

Julie pull out a knife and stone it in the cows mans
throat and   The cow man drop to his
knees. As both men did the same.
Angela shoot the three of them and their bodies melted
between the crack of the ground.   Whats taking Bob so long?
Heather asked.   As she stand on guard.   The truck
is no'longer in use. We need to find Bob. Said Angela.

Jessica arrive in New-york, where her grandfather Vander wise
live.
Get that Horse off the side-walk!! Shouted the voice of a woman.
Jessica look around and see nobody. Im up here!
The woman said. Jessica look's up, and see
a woman with short black hair and about in her mid 60's,
Wearing black glasses. As she stick her head out of the window.
 Sorry, but I can park where'ever I may. Said
Jessica. As she enter the Apartment and go up to the
second floor. when she arrive on the second floor,
A bad odor approach her nose. What is that Odor smell?

She asked her'self. Did The church see you? Asked an older
Mexican man with short black hair. I didnt catch that!
Jessica said in a curious tone. That church is very evil.
Every night, some-one' go missing. He said.
How long ago was this? Jessica asked. Last night!
when

Tasha suppose to come back from work".   He replied.
Im waiting!!   shouted the same woman as before.
Jessica fan her nose and walks away. { Just then, James
stand' head to head with Lamar… ready to draw.
James blink one time and Lamar

shoot' him dead. Lee
defeated all three demons. As Black mary, Mocking, and santics
was all thats left.   Swiftly, The S antics take out their wooden
sticks and start throwing them at the people of the pub.
Lee step infront of the people .   No, we
got this". One of the men said. As they step infront
of Lee. care'ful, you'll be killed! cried Michelle. The people
of the pub ignore what she said and start charging .
Hold your positions!! Shouted Mocking.   The santics change
their sticks into spike bats.   As the crowd of pubs was
getting close, Mocking fill her eyes with anger and spits out
blood. Attack!!! Mocking shouted. Swiftly, the Santics
start swinging their bats and blood was being splatter all over

place.   Saoirse fire her gun at the Santics and the bullets
vanish inside their body's.   As The people was Defenseless.
See   what im talking about?
They dont stand a chance. Said Lee.   Ready to do this?
Lamar asked. Im ready". Lee said.   Save my mother
for me!   Michelle said. You have no powers". Camron said.
How do I get powers like theses guys? Michelle asked.
Just close your eyes". Said Lee. Michelle close her eyes
and Lee kiss her on the lips and walk away. Michelle
opens her eyes and rub her lips and smiles.   Feel powerful?
Camron asked. "I think so! Said Michelle. Im not talking about
your lips!" said Camron.   Suddenly, a white Horse appear
and bows.   Where did this Horse come from? Michelle

asked.   I think it wants you to climb on!
Camron   said. Michelle rub the Horse   head and climb
on its back, and The Horse rides off.

Michelle holds on for dear life. As mocking see her daughter
and aim her sword at her. As she
Prepare to strike her off. But the Horse knock
Mocking down and the sword fall out of her hand.
You tried to kill me mother!

Michelle said. Go ahead, kill me!!! Shouted Mocking. Get out of
my sight". Said Michelle As she turn away and lower
her sword. Suddenly, Mocking pull out a short knife
and try to stab Michelle in her back. But the Horse raise
on its two feet and Michelle turns around and put the
sword through her mother heart and Mocking turn
into stone and vanish. Evil is over and now
im free! Shouted Michelle. Next, she look at the two
guards who'd followed her and they both surrender. By
putting their hands up. Want to work for me?
Michelle asked. The guards nod their head yes. Guard this
ship. Said Michelle. The guards agree' and guard the ship.

CHAPTER : 27

Everything went back to normal. As The people
came' back to life.
Skippy, Lamar, and the rest aboard the ship. I want to
come with you! Said Saoirse. Uncle Robert will be very
Angry". Said Drew.   Let him, im tired of this normal life!
Saoirse said. Come aboard!   Said Lee.   Drew look
around and follow his sister on board. after Dublin,
Michelle and Camrons' journey ends, and they wave goodbye.
As the ship sail off into the distance.   "That was one
crazy adventure! Said Camron.   As she put her arm around
Michelle and they both walks   home.

{Jessica knock on Apartment 217 and the door open.
My dear Jessica! Said Vander wise.   As he hug her.
Hello grandpa!   Said Jessica. As her boots light up.
Vander close   the door. As he invite her into the Apartment.
What a beautiful place! Said Jessica.   As two cars was
racing inside the picture.

what people dont know is… cars are magic as well! Said Vander.
that's very creative!   She replied.

what brings you here? Vander asked. My house was burned
down! Said Jessica.   You know, most people dont think
witches have good deeds ...until they need your help!
Said Vander. " that's what I was trying to tell them!
Said Jessica.
Suddenly, everything went back to normal. As

A shadow of a person, knock on the door.
Knock". Knock". are you home Vander? Asked the
same woman Jessica saw earlier. Vander use silent magic. As She hear
no response and leave.
Vander remove from his position and walk' into
the kitchen.   I saw that woman earlier. Said Jessica.
What did she say to you? Vander asked.   For me to
move my Horse. Jessica replied. Vander sit at the table
and look' out of the window.   Whats wrong grandpa?
Jessica asked. That woman isnt a woman".   Vander said.
What is she then? Jessica asked. As she pours her a
glass of orange juice and grab her two blue- berry muffins

and sit at the table with Vander. Demons has many ways

of tricking people. The church thats across the street,
can make things happen. Even take over your life.
Vander said. An older mexican man said… a woman
name Tasha vanished. Said Jessica. yes, it was three days ago.
Vander said. I want to put a stop to this! Said Jessica.

"I'll upgrade your powers and we'll head out tonight! Said
Vander. at night, Jessica was giving purple wings and
two axes, as weapons. while Vander use a pipe as a weapon.
Jessica gave Vander a weird look". "This pipe is magical!
Vander said. How's that? Jessica asked. Lowering her
axes. "grab hold to this pipe". Said Vander.
Jessica pass her second axe to Vander and grab hold
to the pipe and they both teleport from the Apartment and
 to the Church. That was spooky!! said Jessica.
As she was amazed! See, I dont lie! Said Vander. As he
give back her axe. Jessica look around and
no'one was in sight and she push the door open.

strong wind with silence, approach their face's and the door close
 behind them. Vander try to open the door but it was jam for good.
we're stuck here! Said Vander. It know's we're here. Jessica said.

Just then, Lee and his friends was in the process of leaving
England until, three ships surround them and
it was The police. What brings you
all here? One of the guards asked. we're going to
visit my uncle! Lee said. As a plank slide
on their ship and five guards aboard at the same time.
Look, we're not looking for any trouble!
Said Lamar. My uncle's in charge of Dublin and he'll
be mad… if he knew you'd approach us! Said Saoirse.
And who is your uncle? The cop asked. Robert Dublin".
Said Drew. Suddenly, the cop look at his guards and
start laughing. Saoirse put both hands on her guns and look
At Lee. Lee shake his head no and remain silent.

The cop touch her face and put his hand back to him'self.

its against the law to touch her! Said Drew. As he tighten
his fist and give a mean look. "I am the law boy, and
I can do whatever I want!!   The cop said.   Suddenly,
Drew strike the cop in the face and The guards shoot
him three times and Drew fall on the ship deck.
Swiftly, Lee cause three of the ships to burn and sink in
the ocean. You shot my brother!!! Saoirse shouted.
he's Alive. Said Lee.   You dont know that! Saoirse

shouted.   Lee take a knee and put his hand over Drew's body
and his body begin to heal. As the the bullets push
out of his chest.   The cop was shock and pull a gun on
Lee.   I knew you had to be a wizzard!
The cop said.   Drop your gun partner". Said Lamar. As
him and Skippy had the cop at gun point. you're making

a big mistake. Said the cop. As he drop the gun.
Get off this ship, if you wanna live! Said Skippy. you'll
pay for this! Said the police man. As he jump off the
ship and swim in the ocean, and the ship sail to
the north.   {Jessica and Vander, was confronted by two pit
bulls and they both was the size of a lion.   Jessica hold both
axes in the air and Vander's pipe was lit
with fire. One pit charge at Vander and the other at Jessica.

Jessica use her axe to kill the pit-bull and it falls on its
side. Next, she pull her axe out of the pit
and throw' it at the next pit.
Vander start hitting the pit in
the head, in a heart beat.   Its dead!!   Shouted Jessica.
Vander stop and look at Jessica. As his eyes was filled
with fear. Jessica   pull her axe out the pits body and
check on her grandfather. You dont have to do this! I
can take this misson alone! Said Jessica. A wizzard is

never scared! Said Vander. As he see' a statue
of mary, standing over a Bath- tub. Open up!
Vander said. Suddenly, blood pours out of Marys eyes and
fill the tub.   I thought the mother
of Mary was suppose to be good? Asked   Jessica.
I was catholic once, and there was things going on I couldnt
understand until this day". Vander said. All of a sudden..
the statue of Mary - including the bath-tub falls   through the floor
and made a big hole.
 Somebody help!   "cried" The voice of a woman.

 That must be Tasha! Said Vander. As he jump
into the hole and then Jessica.
A new Journey begins for Joana and Law, as they walk   up the
 road.   Suddenly, a truck pull up beside them and it was
 a caucasian man
with a santa beard, and wearing a cowboy hat with two women
in their 30's and two men around the same age , sat in the
back of the truck. "You folks   lost? He asked .
Yes!". Joana replied. As her and law was sweating from the sun.

where you folks headed? The man asked.   Father, Look!!
Shouted a woman with long brown hair, and wearing rip shorts
and white shoes.   Joana and Law turns to only see
a creature with a long swinging beard, charging at them.
Shoot the darn thing!! he shouted.   The women and men
shoot at the creature But the creature was still charging
at them.

Its too paranormal   for them!! shouted
Joana. Law take up his Hammers and charge at the creature.
What is he doing? the man asked Joana.   you'll see!

Joana said.   Vander and Jessica landed hard on a cold floor.
Over here!!   Shouted
Tasha.   As The voice come from the north.
Vander point the pipe toward's the north and there he see'
a giant bat, mix with a dog face.   Let her go,
You demon!! shouted Vander. The Bat open its mouth
and Vander jump in its mouth.
Spit my grand-father out!! Shouted Jessica. The Bat
laugh and spit' on Jessica. Jessica fly into the air
and throw one of her axe into the bat eyes.
The bat scream in The voice of a wicked woman, Causing the
church to shake.   Inside the Bats mouth, sat a
forest and it's covered by monks and Trees.
Im right here!   Said Tasha.   As the trees

hold' her by the arm's.   Vander try running past them
 but the Monks ambush him. Tasha become
worried".   As the trees   start "laughing. Swiftly, Vander knock

180

CHAPTER : 28

them off by the power of his pipe. Tasha was set free.
.as the trees and the Monks start bleeding.   Vander
see's two hearts of blood and put his hand on Tashas
shoulder. Tell Jessica I love her!   Vander said. With a
sad look on his face.   We can get out of here!   Tasha
said. Vander turn away and   knock Tasha out the demons
mouth and strikes" the two hearts with his pipe.
where's my grand-father?   Jessica asked.   He said he love
you! Tasha said.   He cant do this alone!   Jessica cried.
As she try to fly in the creatures mouth.   But she was
knock back down.   Get out of here! Shouted Vander.   As the
creatures body was smoking.   Jessica grab Tasha and fly
out of the hole and out of the church.   Suddenly, the church

explode as the axes was still with Jessica. "You two should
be ashame of your'selves, im calling the cops!! Shouted a
fat color lady.   Jessica climb on her Horse and pull
Tasha on, and ride' off into the sky.
The color woman stand speech'less.   "Hello, Are you still there?
The operator asked.   {Bob was being

found.   As he stood by the gas pump.   Is everything
okay?   Julie asked.   You wasnt suppose to follow me!!
Bob shouted.   You doing alright??
Heather asked.   How's my truck? Bob asked.   It was
knock over from us fighting this weird... cow man.
Julie said. You broke my truck! said Bob. As he
show his teeth and walk' away.   Where you going?
Angela asked.   he's not him'self".   Said Heather.
This area isnt safe. Be on guard.   Julie said . All of a
sudden... Bob appears with three different men and
all of them were running at Julie, Heather, and Angala.
Stop where you are!!! shouted
Angela. Pointing the gun at them.   Suddenly, they vanish.
Where do you suppose they went? Julie asked. Holding her

Bow and arrow infront of her. lets stand back to back".
Said Angela. As strong wind blow through their hairs.

wait, do you hear that?   Heather asked.
Bob re-appear, and put Julie in a head'lock. Heather punch
him in the face and Julie shoot' him with three
arrows, and he explode with rage.   What a nice performance!"
 they said..   As they re-appears as well.

Heathers   hair light up, and she open the ground with her hands
and they falls   into the hole.
"Seem   like,   you three are going down! Said Julie.
With a smile on her face.
Next, she close the ground with her hand's. What's our next step?
Angela asked. I thought we was going to Las'vegas? Heather
asked. we'll have to keep stopping for food and gas".
Said Angela. I think I found three motor Bikes!" said Julie.

Law smash the creatures head and
 jump on the back of the Truck.   Suddenly, more
creatures crawl from out of the ground and The man accelerate".
Who are you?
Joana asked.   "You can call me mean, John!   Said John.
Looking through the rear view mirror and see nothing".
Im Joana, and my friend back there
is Hammer law!".   Said Joana. "Glad to have him for a weapon!

Said John. As he dtive down a dirt road, that lead to
a cabin. Whats this place? Joana asked.   Our home!
John said.   As he park the truck infront of the cabin and
it was surrounded by woods and grass , that
reach the sky. Law jump off
the truck.   Two chairs was being eating and the stairs
was being torn off!   A creature's been here! one
of the men said.   As they check into the cabin.   How do you
people stay safe?   Joana Asked.   "Keeping the door locked!

said John. At night, dinner was being cook.
 Who are these people?
Joana asked.   "they're   my kids!   John said. As he was
cooking on the stove.   Seem like they been taught well!
Said Law.   "Taught   them   to shoot   and take care of themselves!

said John.
{The work of Pitts has been incomplete,
 and he sits in a purple chair and thought to himself.   "Whats something I can create more power-ful??
he asked himself.
Maybe a son! Said an Australian woman with dark blonde
hair and wearing a purple suit.   How did
you get down here? Pitts asked.   The king of darkness
let me in! She said.   Only im the king of darkness around
here! Said Pitts.   "Not the only one! She said.
Get to the point". Said Pitts. I heard the news that your
moons was killed, and some of the creations!".
So.. im here to help you start a new world order".
She said.   Whats your name, and what proof do you have?
Asked. Pitts.
You can call me.. Azabel ziggy! She said. As she make
the blood dry up and it change into a scottish man. His skin's
white as snow, and hair long and black. Hello, father? He said.

what should you name your son?   Azabel asked.
His name shall be Patrick!   Said Pitts.
I want a suit to wear, father.   Patrick said In a creepy tone.
Pitts put Patrick into a black suit.   Looking love'ly
there! Said Azabel. As she touch Patricks jacket.
Hand off, I dont want it dirty! Said Patrick.   What a mean
man! Said Azabel as she walk away and stand next to Pitts.
You have the power to destroy any-one and everything,
my son. Said Pitts.   I wont let you down father! Said
Patrick. As he vanish from Pitts and Azabels sight.

Whats my mission? Azabel asked.   Your mission is to
look for a woman name Abby and kill her.
Said Pitts.   Why do you want this woman dead?
Asked Azabel. Because she's gifted! Said Pitts.
That make sense".
Azabel said. As she climb up on the Horse. " What a beautiful
 Horse you have!". Said Pitts. The star's symbolize power
and strength! Said Azabel.

188

CHAPTER : 29

as she ride off into the portal of blood.
{three of John son's, was loading the truck with tree's
 until they hear a disturbing scream} ahhhhhhhhh!!!"
in a panic,
They jump inside the truck and one
of them try to start it.   But it would'nt start.   The

Truck lowered with creatures and Patrick appear
and make them go away.   "Thank you sir!
One of them said.   As he get   out of the truck.   Its too
dangerous out here".   Patrick   said. As he look around
and back at them, in a non reactive way.   For your reward,
we welcome you to our Cabin!"   Said the man who confronted
Patrick.   When they made it back at the Cabin,
he calls for his father.   Father?".   John come running
out of the Cabin to see his sons and Patrick
with them.   Whats going on? John asked.   This man saved

us, from those creatures. Said his son. "glad to meet you
John! Said Patrick. As he shake Johns hand and
let go. Strong grip there! Said John. As he give Patrick
 a punch on the shoulder. " I work out more often!
Patrick said. Thanks for saving my sons! Would
you like something to eat? John asked. I rather sit
down! Said Patrick. Make your'self at home! "Come
guys, supper is ready! Said John. As they leave
Patrick's sight. who's in the living room? Joana asked. Patrick
the Hero! Said John. serving
their plates. You have to becare'ful of who you let in the
Cabin! Said Joana. "that man saved our lives" Said

one of his sons. While Patrick sit in the living room,
he signals fo the creatures to attack,
by opening the door. Multiple creatures enter the Cabin
and Patrick point in the kitchen. Suddenly, the
creatures start attacking everyone and Patrick smiles
and leave out of the Cabin.

Everything become silent. As he stand out-side.
In between   times, the ship arrive in Denmark. As they sail
on dry land. You must go to Arabian.   Said Cindy.
Whats going on? Asked Lee.   Cindy wants us to travel to
Arabia!   Said Lamar. "You know what to do" Lee said.
As he shake both of their hands and depart ways.
Whats that all about? Saoirse asked. you'll find out.
Said Lee.   Look like we're in Denmark! Drew said.
As The voice of a beautiful woman singing, approach their
ears. where's that coming from? Lee asked.   Sound
like a music "festival!   Saoirse   replied.
As she run ahead of them to climb the stairs,

that lead to another town. When she make it to the top,
there was ten of thousands of people at the music festival".
Just what I thought!"
Said Saoirse . As Lee and Drew   arrive and
thats when they see the music festival. Ready for some fun?"

CHAPTER : 30

The night has fallen in Arabia.
As Albert and Abby bare'ly escape the the under cave of the curse.
Do you think we she should have stolen that golden bird?
Abby asked. "Not to worry my child, you'll be more richer!
Said Albert.

As he's the king of Albujaru.   Azabel   watch from
above and she throw a silver star in the sand.

Suddenly, Albert and Abby fall off their Horses and
Azabel   dismount her Horse and start kicking Albert
aggressive'ly in the rib side. Abby push Azabel off her father
and help him up.   Suddenly, Azabel turn into a she-beast
with three wings and two heads, Her body also turn into
a bear and dragon.   Their eyes was full of fear.
What do you want? Abby asked.
Alber run and pull a sword from his Horse, to confront
Azabel.   Its not you I want, its Abby!!!" Azabel shouted..

you're not killing my daughter!!!"
Shouted Albert. Dont do it father!! Abby shouted.
Albert look back at Abby, with tear's in his eyes and
he said... I love you! Swiftly, Azabel fly through his body
and Albert vanish. the sword drop infront of her.
Abby eyes fill with tears. As her father was gone!}
Strong wind picks up, and Abby grab the
sword and jump up on her Horse and rides away".
Where are you going Abby?
asked Azabel. As she chase after her, on wings.

Abby was almost near the city. As she was ten feet
away. Azabel fly and knock Abby off her
Horse and her body hit the sand. Abby get's up and attack
Azabel with a sword, and Azabel block with
a sword" and kick Abby in the stomach. Abby hold
her hand on her stomach . As she was in pain".

Out of nowhere, a rope lasso was throw around Azabels neck
and was pull down. Next, Lamar jump into the air
and shoot Azabel in the arm. Azabel spin
into the sand. you alright? ? Lamar asked.
As he help her get up. That thing killed my father!" Cried
Abby. We can not talk here! Lamar said.
My home is there". Said Abby. As she points in the north.
Suddenly, the ship explode". Get her to safety!! Shouted Skippy.

As they start running together   {The trees bow before
Patrick. As he stand in the middle of the road. mission
accomplish, father! Patrick

Said. As he fly into the sky.   Great job! now I want
you to go to india. Said Pitts.   What do you have in
mind? Patrick asked.   Find three of my brothers, and use
my name only. Said Pitts. Understood father! Said Patrick.
Bodies of creatures was laying all over the floor. As

Law, Joana, and a woman survived. To her surprise, The family
was destroy.   I would love to get my hands on that bastard!!
shouted Law.   Whoever he is…. not a normal person!
Said Joana. As she walk into the living
room. Why did they bring him here?
The woman asked.   Your brothers was too trusting".

Joana replied.
All of a sudden… The Cabin start splitting in half.
We need to get out of here!! the woman shouted.
As she grab the key and run out-side. "Our truck!
she cried. Suddenly, the tree' block the road. Lets run the
other way.

said Law.   As they run through the woods.
{The gate was opened by the guards, and they enter the gate.
What happened? Safina asked. who's queen of the Kingdom.

The Monster attack us and killed father!"   cried Abby.
Revenge!! The Guard shout. It's too powerful". Abby said.
Lamar and Skippy approach and the guard draw
his sword.   Dont, they're my friends! Said Abby. Where
are they from? Asked Safina. They saved me
from the monster!". Abby said. Im Lamar! Said Lamar.
My name's Safina, and I'm the queen of this kingdom
and city! She said.   Your daughter's not safe here. Said Skippy.
Why would a monster attack my family? Safina asked.
Because your daughter is the next gifted one and
evil don't like it. Said Lamar. Im leaving at Dawn. Said Abby.

CHAPTER : 31

200

at night, Abby pack her bag and put it on the carpet
that has writing's on it.
Your room is hooked up! Said Skippy. As he saw guitars
and posters of famous Actors". Suddenly,
Abby pour water on three carpets and they start to levitate. You have flying carpets?? Lamar asked.
Im gonna miss you! Said Safina. As she grab Abby
hands and touch her face. Dont be sad mother, I'll
come back! Said Abby. As she hug her mother and
sit on the carpet.   The door blow open and

Abby blows her mother a kiss and fly into the
sky. {Safina watch out of the, door until her daughter
 was out of sight.} How does it feel to leave your
home? Lamar asked. I have to do what I have to do!
Abby said. Suddenly, The wind blow strongly.
she's back again. Said Skippy. As he pull out a gun
and scan' around.   {Azabel was nowhere
in sight.} "Maybe its the wind!
Abby said. To be a powerful warrior, you have to
tell the different's!" Said Lamar. How? Abby asked.
Azabel lands on Abby. Thought your can
escape!!!" Azabel shouted. Trying to throw

Abby off the carpet. Skippy shoot her in the back five times and
she vanish. You alright? Lamar asked. Yes". Abby said...
Holding her heart". we're taking you to cindy. Lamar
said. Azabel return back to pitts, "screaming" in pain.
Pitts remove the bullets out of her back and The body
heal it'self.   These bullets are made
of iron. They're protecting her. Said Azabel.
You told me you was powerful enough to kill them! Pitts
said.   It was the cowboys".   Said Azabel.

Suddenly, Pitts grab his heart and drop on his knee.
What's wrong? Azabel asked. I want life!
Said Pitts. What do you mean? Azabel asked.
Master orange once said... if evil dont take a life,
us dark'ness become weak,
And so will you! Said Pitts.   What should I do
to keep us strong?   asked Azabel.
Patrick's out looking for my brother's, and you must go to
Denmark. Said Pitts.   What if she's no use to me?
Azabel asked. my brothers will

take over.   Said Pitts. Should they bring her here?   Azabel
asked.   Look for a church and kill anyone you see!
Said Pitts.   Azabel   vanish from his sight. "Leaving him

with a smile on his face.

In the festival, the music ends with a solo guitar and
The Danish woman smile to the round of applause".
Your voice's amzaing! Said Lee.   Thank you!   She said.
You should be a singer! Said Drew.   Thats my goal!
She replied.   "How long you been singing?   Lee asked.
Since I was little! She said.   Very beautiful!
Said her grand-father.   As he hug her and look at   the
three of them.   This is my grand-pa Bob.   She said.
With her arm around his waist and smiling with a love'ly
smile.   "I see that you met my grand- daughter, Karen!
Said Bob. As he was wearing brown shorts and a t-shirt
that match his shirt.   she's very talented!   Said Saoirse.
Suddenly, Drew see' a man carrying bags of cotton candy.
May I have a bag of cotton candy, please?.. Drew asked
Thats gonna cost you! Said a skinny man with messed up
teeth and has oil on his face, with long grey hair.   I dont
have any money". Drew said.   The man leave Drew' sight...

by walking into the distance. Drew return to his sister and aske
for a bag of cotton candy. Where do you see cotton
candy at? Saoirse asked. A skinny man was carrying
them all". Drew said. What does he want?"
Karen asked. Cotton candy. Saoirse said. that'll be
one dollar!" Bob replied. As he reache' into his pocket and
give him a dollar, and he leave' their sight .
Im sorry for his manners." Said Saoirse. Thats okay,
hes excited! Bob said. Wouldnt you two want
to have some fun? Karen asked. I can use a long
break! Said Lee. Lets get some tickets! Said Bob.

As him and Lee walk off. Drew found the
man sitting down and he run toward's him. I'll take
a bag of cotton candy, please! Do you have money this time?
The man asked. Drew show him The dollar bill and the
man gives him a bag of cotton candy. thanks, sir!
Said Drew. As he turn away. Swiftly, the man "hit" Drew
on the head and put him in The van. People are

so easy to lure! Said the man. As he leave away from the van. Its taking your brother so long".
.said Karen". you're right,
Im going to find my brother. Said Sairose. leaving

her sight. Saoirse walk through a crowd asking...

have they seen her brother. Out of 10 people said no.
looking for your brother Drew? Azabel asked.
Do you know where he is.. ? Saoirse asked. He was put
in a van, Azabel said. Saoirse
see's a black van and run over to it.
When she made it to the van, she open
the door and see her brother laying on his side.
What are you doing? Asked a cop. "My brother was put
in this van! Cried Saoirse;. Did you see the man who
did it? The cop asked. I just got here , when my brother
went missing! She said. What happened?? Drew asked. As he seem
confused and he jump out the Van. Did you see the man

who did it? Asked the cop. It was a skinny man with bad teeth and long grey hair". Said Drew. Grabbing his cotton candy and leaving with Saoirse. You need to stop walking off! Said Saoirse. Im not a little kid anymore! Drew said. In a angry tone. you're not ready to be mature! Saoirse replied. Drew walk ahead of her to meet up with Leeporder. After that, everyone get on the ride.

After the ride, food, and drinks, they decided to call it a day. As the five of them was worn out. "Wouldnt you three like to come to our place? Bob asked. why not!". Lee said. As the five of them get in the truck and left the festival behind. Azabel wait for the right time to meet her. Suddenly, a group of women start laughing and chatting. As they sat on a bench, drinking and eating.

want to become famous? Azabel asked? "You have to
be kidding me! Said a youth'ful womam, with long braids
in her hair. Suddenly money appear on their laps.
The

girls become shocked!". As they stare with a big smile.
We   accept! Said the black woman with braids.
So they arrive at the house and it was surrounded by land
and no trees. The house also sat by a one lane
 road. What a large house! Saoirse said.
As she approach the open porch and sit on the swing
that's only for three people. I can see buildings   and
lands from here! She said in a most amazing'ly   tone.
"Sometimes   I sit on this swing to write lyrics! Karen
said. I do garden work, on my free time!
Said Bob.   Lee   sits on the porch and stare   at
the land.   We bare'ly had any rest. Said Lee.
Where you guys from? Bob asked. Dublin Ireland!
Saoirse replied. My friends brother, live there! Bob said.
we'll be hitting the road soon. Lee said. staring down
the one lane road.   No, you three can stay with us".
I like you guys! Bob said.   "Okay! Said Lee. As he shake

CHAPTER : 32

{it was a long Journey from Las-vegas, as Patrick appear
on the road.. causing them to fall off their
mo-bikes. Angela' was hurt from a serious accident.

what's the deal? Heather asked. Patrick stares at Julie
and pull her close to him. Whats your name? He
asked Julie. Julie! She said. Leaning away from him.
Let her go! Said Angela. As she points a gun at Patrick.
Patrick gives Angela a very cold stare and the gun explode
in Angelas face and she was knock all the way
back where she came from. That was our best friend!
Said Julie. As she struggles to get away from him.
Patrick put her to sleep. By staring into her eyes.
Suddenly, Heather fly and kick him in the face.
Patrick smiles and punch her to the ground, and vanish with
Julie in his arms. When Heather got up, they was gone.

Julie woke up and saw Patrick, sitting   above her head.
"Welcome to Vegas! He said. As they sat in a large
hotel room, filled with black dressers and
queen size beds, with black silk covers... along with objects
that match. There too was a bed that sat by the
window, where they can see the strip from above .
 Beautiful, isnt it? Asked Patrick.
As he look at the view with her. When Julie was looking
at the view of the strip, she noticed she was wearing a black dress.
How did you know, and why am I wearing a black dress? She asked.
"Its a dream for a wedding! Patrick said. Who are
you? Julie asked. My name's Patrick and I am
the son of darkness". He said. Touching her face, with cold hands.
Suddenly, she get off the bed and run' out the room. {Hurry boy!!

shouted Pitts.   I'am sorry, father. Said Patrick .   As he vanish.
Both security   enter   the   room   and see   no-one.
Julie   becomes   shocked. As Patrick   was   nowhere to be found.
Are you sure he was in here?   Asked security.
I'm sure! Said Julie. As she look confused".   Heather
hit the ground and saw a vision of Julie in a beautiful
Hotel room.   Shes in vegas! Heather said
to herself   flying off into   the distance.
Julie sit at the table wondering… who was that guy!?
Angela's sat with her back, against the gas'station building
and her face was damage from the gun explosion.
.Angela   slowly move   her fingers and Legs…
Until she hear   The voice of a woman.   you alright,
officer?   Angela passed out.   Next, Angela woke up and
saw two older couple, starting at her.   Where

am I ? Angela asked.
We bought you here, and cleaned your face! Said the mystic
woman. Angela try removing from the table and she falls off.
You want to be careful dear! Said the womans husband.
As he help' her to a chair and she sit down.
Why do I feel so weak? Angela asked. Well… I had to
put something in ya! She said to Angela, with
a wicked smile. Wanted to make sure you we took car of
you! He said. Suddenly, The room become small. As Angelas
vision, become poor. Lets put her in the basement.
The woman said to her husband. But, what if she scream?
He asked. she's too doped up for that! she replied!
Suddenly, her husband pick up Angela and carry her to
the basement. Make sure you tie her up, really good!!
she shouted from above the basement stairs.

{Julie was sleeping on the bed, until she woke up to a sound of pounding on the wall. Julie sat up and listen close'ly.
Once again, the pounding approach her ears.
Next, she get out of bed and walked towards the door
and open it. and When she peek into the hall, there
she saw people with sharp claws and wolf heads.

All of a sudden.. they saw her watching them and charge at
her. Julie swiftly close and lock the door.
Heather arrive in Las'vegas.
As people was turning into creatures. What happened to
this place? Heather asked her'self. As her feet touch
the ground, the people start sniffing in the air and
she tip-toe through the entrance of the hotel.
When she make it inside, the front lobby was empty silence.
Is anybody here?! She shouted. Sound of foot-steps approach

213

ears and she run and hide behind the desk.
Julie open the door. As they was no-longer in sight.
Thought I heard somebody! She said to her'self.

Angela was tied to a chair and her mouth was covered
with a scarf. You must be hungry! Said the man.
As he turn into a war-lock and walk down stairs.
His head was covered with hair and his body was made of
pig. Angelas eyes grow large.
You dont have to be scared". I bought you something to eat!
He said. Putting the tray on the floor.
All of a sudden.. the Warlocks head was split in-half and
there appear Gabe. Angela start moving around.
Shhhhh... dont want to make noise". Gabe said. As he untie
her and she swiftly hug him. Im so glad to see
you! She said. My car's waiting out-side.! Gabe replied.
Suddenly, the basement door open. You alright, Terry?
She asked. Im alright dear, Im feeding our dinner!
Gabe said. Wait, why's the chair empty? She asked.
She tried to scream and I ate her. Gabe replied.
Suddenly, she jump down the base-ment stairs and
Gabe hit her on the head, and she falls on the floor.
We thought you was dead! Said Angela. Zack and I
will never die! Said Gabe. I lost Heather and Julie!
   Angela said. I suppose they're in Las- vegas. He
replied. {Heather peek over the desk, to see human'
with wolf heads. Impossible".. She said to her'self. peeking

over the desk.   Angela and Gabe arrive in Vagas. As the
streets was flooded with people, with wolf heads.
How did this happen? Angela asked.
Dark magic was put on this city. Said
Gabe.   Look. Angela said.   When Gabe look to his
left, he see a group of people, approaching the car.
All of a sudden.. a gun set's off and   Zack   approach their
sight.   What took you so long, my boy!?   Gabe asked.
Cindy wanted me to do something   for her! Zack replied.
As he shoot at the people and they become   normal
again.   That's all we have to do? Angela asked. As she
gets out the car and start shooting. The people in the
lobby, runs outside. Heather   jump over the desk
to see who's outside. Heather!!?   Shouted Julie. As she
hug her.   Im so happy to see you, and you look different!!
Heather said.   I dont have my weapons anymore".
Said Julie.   Where could they be?   Heather asked.   Patrick
must of ditch them somewhere.   Julie replied to Heather.
Before Haeather   could speak, Julie gained black wings.
Thats   really sick!! Heather said. I have black wings?   Julie

TURN   THE   NEXT   PAGE....

{if you have'nt put this book down, you're Adventurous than I thought".
You   may proceed".}

asked.   Suddenly, two security's come walking through
the entrance. Julie grab Heathers hand and run
up-stairs.   The owner return to the front desk,
 unaware. seem's like Vegas is back to normal!
Said Gabe. Its beautiful! Said Heather. As she look
at the view of the   strip. I cant believe we are here!
Said Julie. As she put her arm around Heathers
neck.   Heather look at Julie and smile.
 Suddenly, some'one knock at the door.
Julie walk towards the door and open it. And it was
Gabe and Zack.   You did'nt order room service, did ya?!
Gabe asked.   As he hug Julie.   "Welcome to Vegas!
Said Heather.   "Thank you very much, and im up for a casino!
Said Gabe.
So   there'fore, Gabe, Zack, Julie and Heather, regroup and
head out the door".   But, do they Journey
end here??}

Patrick arrive' in India.   As a crowd of people stood and stared.
Im looking for three Jewish men.   Said Patrick.
I can show you to their King-dom.   Said an older
man who's wearing a white robe   and has a long black beard.
what's your name son?   He asked Patrick.
Patrick,   son of Pitts.   Said Patrick.   I didnt know Pitts had
a son!".   Said the man.   You knew my father?
Patrick asked.   Yes, I helped him create   the moons.
He replied.   The moons are dead".   Said Patrick.
How so?   He asked.
A woman name cindy, hired some punks   to kill them!   Said Patrick.
How come Pitts never mention this?   He   asked.
As   they   walk up the stairs.
Cool Kingdom!   Said Patrick.

In past time's..
Joana, Law,   and the woman, come to a dead end.

This was'nt suppose to happen! She said to Joana and Law.
Step away from the bridge!
said an old creepy man, carrying a pumpkin with a light
inside it. Law and Joana turn around and see
a creepy old man dressed, in all black.   Where did you
come from? Joana asked.   I come from a town called
Graves and Hallow.   He   said.   This is the land of grass
and trees!   Said Law.   Not any-more".
This land play   tricks on people".   He replied.   You're   telling
me that my father bought a cabin that was never here???

she asked.   All of a suudden...

The daughter of John' was dragged off the cliff.
She   screams until   her voice is heard, no'more.
We must get off the road".   The   man   said.   What are you

talking about?   Joana   asked.
Run, Now!   Shouted   the man.   As they   blend   together".

Patrick   arrive at the entrance   of the Kingdom and the man
knock four times.   who's to   knock at the door?
Asked The voice of a man.   A young man wish to see you.
The man replied.   Swiftly,   the door open and there stood
three jewish men. My father Pitts, need your help.
Said Patrick.   We'll   go to through the black mirror. Said
one of the Jewish men, who wore   dark glasses.
I'll leave you to your journey!   Said the man.   As he leave
Patricks   sight and walk down the stairs.
When Patrick enter the Kingdom, it was filled with gold
and statue' of Lions.   Come Patrick, your father a-waits".
Said one of the jewish men.

Walk through. The jewish man said. Patrick
step inside the mirror and was back where he came from.
"You did well, my son!   Said Pitts.
What seem to be the problem brother?   The moons are gone
and I need another soul to live!   Pitts said. Just wait until
what happens, with Azabel!   Said Patrick.

As a table and four chairs   appear, with a bottle of red wine ontop.
Anyone up for a game of cards?   Patrick asked.
there's time for a game of cards!   Said Pitts. As him and his
brothers sit at the table and start playing.   "No cheating!
Said Patrick.

221

CHAPTER : 33

222

{Malisa end's back at her Apartment, not knowing what happened
to Lee or Heather.   Are you lost, pretty lady?! Asked
a man with a long brown beard and wearing all black.

he's only trying to talk to ya!". Said one of the men, who was
behind him.   I better get home". Malisa said. As she rush
through the entrance of the Apartment.   The man decided
to follow her, as he walk through the entrance. Malisa run
in her Apartment and closed the door.
The man   heard and run   up-stairs.   I know what Apartment
you're in!!   he shouted.   Why are you shouting?   Asked
an older black woman, and she was sitting in a wheel-chair.
Where's that creepy girl?!   He asked. pointing a gun
at her.   The black woman point across the hall.

Trembling in fear".

As he approach Malisas door he hears foot-steps,
climbing up the stairs. Suddenly, he run and
climbed out the window.   When the cops arrive, there was
nobody in sight, Accept the open window. Malisa come
out of the Apartment to give information to the cops.
After the cops left, Malisa went to the diner to eat
lunch and still not knowing what happened to Lee and
Heather. It's as if the time went back". As she
think to her'self.   May I sit here? Asked an old creepy
lady, wearing all grey and in her 60's.
Sure! said Malisa. As she was eating her fries.
the old lady sit down with a tea-cup.
Lost your two friends huh?   The old lady asked.   Malisa
stop eating her fries and shockley stare at the lady.
How did you know what I was thinking?   Malisa asked.

lets just say, a demon is always wise! Said the lady. As
she wink at Malisa and sip her tea.   What's your name?
Malisa asked. You can call me evil!   She replied.
Why such a name?? Malisa asked. Looking at her
in a curious way. you're not the first to ask such a
question!   I call my'self evil because.. kids would always pick

on me and burn me with fire, So I became angry and start

attacking everyone! She said.   Make sense to me!   Said Malisa.
{The man who stalked Malisa, entered the Diner.
Give me hot-dogs and fries! He said.   Malisa move to
the right side of the table and finish eating her burger.}

{Mean-while,   Azabel and The Girls arrive at the catholic church,
as all of them were wearing black and has the
power of blue magic. Are you ready girls?   Azabel asked.
The Girls look at one another and smiles.
Suddenly, Azabel kick the door open and the Pastor stop
preaching.   He's a mexican man with grey hair and
skinny.   Are you here to join the service?   He asked
Azabel.   No, I want this church and your students that's
brain washed by your teachings!   Azabel replied.
"Who are you to come in here and play God??"   shouted the
Monk.   As he sat on the left side of the pastor.

The Girl's threw their powers   at the monk and he
turn into ashes, under a robe. The catholic students
start screaming and crying".   Shut up!!!   Azabel shouted.
everybody   remain silent". I dont know
who you are and what you want} But you need to leave".
Said the pastor.   As ten more monks approach the
stage, holding holy water.

Malisa found away to sneak out of the Diner, without being seen.
 as she went back to the Apartment with evil.
Do you know him? Evil asked.   Yes, he was stalking me!
Said Malisa.   Well, I better get going!   Said Evil.
As she open the door.
Do you have anywhere to go?   Malisa asked.
Evil smiles and lick her lips.   Not really!
Evil said. Look, you can stay with me!   Said Malisa.
Thank you, dear!   Said Evil. As she walk into
the living room and pour black salt on the sill.
What are you doing? Malisa curious'ly asked.   Keeping evil away!
Said Evil.   Suddenly, Malisa felt sleepy.
Are you sleepy? Evil asked.   But im not sleepy".
Said Malisa. As she was holding her head.   Get some

sleep, dear! Evil replied. Malisa walk into her room and
lay on the bed.   Evils face turn into a goblin
and she enter Malisas room. As Malisa was fast-
asleep.   Evil climb on her and open her
mouth. Malisa open her eyes and
knock Evil off her and run' out the room.
Next, Malisa try running out the Apartment door,
But the door was locked.   I was'nt gonna hurt you!
Evil said.   As she slow'ly walk out the room.
Stay away from me!". Shouted Malisa. As she run
in the kitchen to grab a knife. All the knive's are gone!
Evil said.   Walking further out the room.   Malisa thought
about the black salt and run into the
living room and sweep the salt from the sill.
Why did you sweep my salt off?! Evil. asked.   As
body turn into a blood goblin.   Suddenly,
a white and brown wand, appear on the sill and Malisa
picks it up.   Next, the wand change black.   I dont understand!
Malisa said.   Put down that wand!!" Evil shouted. Opening her
mouth.   White words appear and read….. White-kingdom
and flick! And the words vanish. Suddenly, Evil
charge at Malisa.   Malisa hold up the wand and shouts...
white-kingdom! And she point the wand at Evil and Evil

explode". As the Apartment was covered in blood.
What did you do?? Asked the owner. As he enter the
Apartment. How did you get in here? Malisa asked.
I have a second key amd you're about to go to jail!
He said. Pulling his cell - phone from out of his pocket. White-kingdom!!
Malisa shouted. As she point her wand and run for her
life. The owner fall-down and could'nt get up.

Joana, Law and the man, board them'selves inside a cabin.
This one's more bigger! Said Law. As the cabin's filled
with candles and old chairs.
What are we running from? Joana asked. Sit down and I'll
tell you both. Said the man.   You didnt give us your
name! Joana said. As her and Law sit at the table.

my name's Ritu. Said Ritu.   Weird name! Joana replied.
Thats why people dont come by here, more often. Said Ritu.
Tell us about this thing. Said Law.   Ritu bring a steel
pot of tea and put it on the table.   That thing we just
ran from is known as... face devil. Said Ritu.
Suddenly, John, daughter, "bang" on the door. Let me in!!"
its our friend! Joana shouted.   Its a trick! Said Ritu.
Let me in!!!   she shouted. Joana run and open the
door and her friend hug Joana and closed the door.
We need to get out of here!!   She shouted   to Joana.
How did you manage to get away? Ritu   asked.
I had to climb my way out! She cried. Come and
drink some tea".   Said Law. As he get up from the chair

and she sit down.   Ritu gives her a weird look and leave from
the table.   At night , when alll was asleep, Ritu
was standing in the woods, holding a red eye.
The woods light up red and the face devil appear. Why'd

you summon me? The devil face asked. As its eyes move around and look at Ritu. Three adults are ready at your service! A woman escaped from me! Said the devil. Shes in the cabin, hiding. Ritu replied. Wake up!" Said John's daughter. what's going on? Asked Law. Look, hurry! She said. Law and Joana creep to the window and saw Ritu talking to a big face devil.

bastard! Said Law. I thought he was good". Said Joana. Go get them for me. Said the devil. Ritu start walking towards the cabin. As Law and Joana hold' their position. Soon as Ritu walk through the door, Law hit him on the head and drag his body away. Next, he exit the cabin to confront the devil face. where's my human? It asked. Right here! Said Law. As he throw a hammer in the devils eyes and it lose his temper".

Swiftly, Law jump into the air. As the Hammer grow large and he smash the devil's head. there's no use of getting out" said Johns daughter. As her head flip

back   and   walk   towards   her.   Joana   dance   a   little
and   bow.   Three   spirits   appear   and   grab
John's   daughter   and   carry   her
into   the   fire   and   she   vanish.   I   found   an   old   chevy   car".
Said   Law.   As   he   turn   the   ignition   and   the   car   start   up.
Its   been   a-while!   Said Joana.   Suddenly,   the   trees
start   growing   hands   and   Joana   jump   into   the   car   and
Law   hit   the   gas,   As   they   drive   off   into   the   distance.

232

CHAPTER : 34

Abby stand before Cindy.
This womans father, was killed by Azabel. Said Lamar.
he's alive! Said Cindy. Abby' eyes was filled with
joy and tears. How do you know? Abby asked.
Turn around". Said the voice of her father. Abby turn
 to only see her father, and she fainted.
Wake up! Said Albert. Abby open her eyes and her
father was still in sight. "you're…. really here!
Said Abby. Im very proud of you! Said Albert. Rubbing
Abbys hair. I told mother. Said Abby.
She need not to worry". When you're fully
awake, your training will be ready. Think you have
the strength? Asked Albert. Oh- father, Im ready!
Abby replied. As she get off the floor and leave Alberts sight.

Mean-while, the apartment's no'longer in sight, as
a cop car was driving down the street.
Malisa act normal, and walk down the Alley.
Next, she get on a green bike and start paddling fast".

After five hr's of paddling, she decided to stop at the store for snacks.
So she lean the bike against   the building, and enter
the store.   Whats going on, Malisa?" Asked Mark.
As he's wearing a blue jump-suit.   Weird things-
going on! Said Malisa.   As she choose which snack she want.
Like what?   Mark asked.   Do you believe
in the supernatural? Malisa asked.   I think so!
He replied.   The door open and in walk the shadow man, carrying
a suit-case.   Can I help you sir?   Mark asked.
The shadow man put the suit- case on   the counter, and Malisa

point the   wand at the shadow-man and he vanish in flames.
What was that??   Mark asked. Believe in it now? Malisa asked.
I sure do!   Said Mark.   As he bag her items   and Malisa
exit' the store.

Abby enter a store that's filled with weapons.
These weapons are base off your personality". Said
Cindy.   As she teleport.   "Im a woman, who
love to carry two swords and a shield!   Said Abby.
As she saw two swords and a shield engraved with hand-writing.

Is this the weapon you wish for? Cindy asked.   It connects
with me well!". Abby replied. Touch the weapon.
Said Cindy.   Abby touch the weapon and the shop change
into a training room, filled with   knights and dummies.
Welcome, to the room of , training warriors!   Said   Cindy.
Pick up your sword.   Said a knight. As he step forward.
Abby pick up the sword and hold it.
Pick up the next one.   The knight said.   Cant believe it, a real Knight!".
Said Abby.   "Block with both swords!   Said Cindy.

suddenly, a Knight perform a single strike: and Abby block
with both swords. Im shocked! Said Cindy.
"My father fought many battles! Said Abby. Do you know
how to use a shield? A Knight asked. Abby drop
the sword and pick up a shield.
Swiftly, the kight swing his sword at Abby
and she block with a shield, by crouching.
Suddenly, a second Knight swing his sword and it "break.
 you're ready! Said the Knight. As they step back into
their position. Cindy hug Abby. "My support is
giving to you! Said Cindy. Am I ready? Abby asked.

As long as you put time in your learning, you'll be fine!
Cindy replied. what's my mission? Abby asked.

The warriors you never met, had completed the biggest missions.
Said Cindy.   As the shop change back to normal.
Wow, where are they now? Abby asked. In different worlds!
Cindy replied.   What are their names? Abby asked.
Gabe, Julie, Zack, Heather, and Leeporder! Said Cindy.

I want mission like theirs! Said Abby. Your missions will be
different from theirs!   Said Cindy.   What do you mean?
Asked Abby. Come, and I'll tell you while we walk! Said
Cindy.   As her and Abby exit the shop.

238

CHAPTER : 35

Bob, Lee, and Drew were chopping wood. As Karen and Saoirse
was inside the house. This is my room! Said Karen.
As they both enters. Its beautiful! Said Saoirse.
As she see posters on the wall.
Are you a fam of the Spice girls? Saoirse asked.
Yes, they're the reason why I wanted to become a singer!
Said Karen. As she turn on the radio.
"There will be an audition held at the great hall today,
starting at 3;00} spoke the sponsor on the radio.
Its 2;59. I better tell my grand-father! Said Karen.

{In the Catholic church, the pastor and other four Monks
were dead. As the catholic students sold their soul to
Azabel for life. Azabel Girls , decorate the church
with eyes and picture's of the beast. "Looks great, im
visiting my friend, and I'll be back. Said Azabel. As a red
light surround her and she Vanish. Azabel teleport to Pitts
The job is done". Said Azabel. "Great. Now you
can go after a soul and my son will take care of the
church. Said Pitts. If this doesnt go well, im passing her
down to you three! Said Azabel. Thats the whole plan!
Said the jewish man . As snakes was crawling on his head.

The red light surround Azabel and she teleport back to
the church. We have work to do! said Azabel.
So   Karen, Bob, and Saoirse left Lee and Drew behind,
as   they was off to an Audition. "Its boring
here! Said Drew. What do you have in mine, man?
Lee asked.   Drew   look around the land and saw
a dark hole.   "Lets check out that hole!
Said Drew. As he run ahead of Lee.   "We have to be care'ful!
Said Lee. As he walk alongside of Drew.
When Drew arrive at the hole, The smell of stink, approach
his nose. Smell' bad!! said Drew.   As he fan his nose.
that's a big hole! Said Lee.   Standing away from the hole.
I agree! Drew replied.   You did a
good job, Drew! Said Lee.   Thanks, man! Said Drew.

somebody up there?   Asked The voice of a little kid?
Are you hurt?   Drew asked.   No, I just want to play down
here! The voice replied! Dont you want to come out?
Lee asked.   No! she said. Drew look at Lee and scratch

his head.   This doesnt seem right!"   Said Lee.
From their surprise: a large face warlock appear,
and Drew punch it in the face.   You shouldnt have
done that!! It shouted. As a hand reach out of its eyes
and grab Drew. Lees right fist light up ,
and he punch the Warlock back into the hole and
the hole become   a grey rock.   "Thanks   for saving me!
Said Drew.   "Welcome!   Said Lee.   As he cant stop
looking   at the rock that use to be a hole.
Come   on Lee, im ready to get out of here! Said Drew.
Lee   and Drew, leaves the black hole behind and never returned.

Bob, Karen, and Saoirse arrive at the hall to only see three
people. Only a few people? Bob asked.
"Im sorry, the three of you didnt make it.!   Said Azabel.

Three of the danish girls put a frown on their faces and
walks away. And who you might be? Azabel asked.
My name's Karen, and I am here for the Audition!
Said Karen. "Hope you got talent, lets see what you got!
Azabel said. As she walk by the chair and sit down.
Karen walk on stage and approach the mic.

If you wanna be my lover,
first you gotta be my friend...

Karen song.   Cut it! Shouted Azabel. As she
get up from the chair to Approach Karen. Karen felt
nervous, As Azabel look her in the eyes, without a
smile.   Did I do something?! Karen asked.   In a nervous
tone. Suddenly, Azabel smiles and hug Karen.
You made it! she said. Karen hug Azabel and start crying".
"Im so proud of you! Said Bob. As he run on stage

and hug Karen.   Now, I want you to sign this contract,
and you'll be on your way! Said Azabel.   Karen takes
the pen sign her name on the dotted line and the Contract
burn and vanish.   "Very weird!   Said Saoirse.   Magic
trick! Azabel replied.   Saoirse hug Karen and said…
im really happy for you!   "Thanks!   Said Karen.
Ready to go? Azabel asked.   Yes!   Said Karen.   Bob kiss
Karen on the fore-head and walk away.   We have a
show tonight!   Said Azabel. As her Girls look at Karen

and laugh".   On the road of fame, Azabel Girls
start waving at everyone, out the limo window.
Want to give it a try? Azabel asked Karen.
I'll just look out the window. Said Karen. The show starts
tonight. Azabel said.   "Im very excited! Said Karen.
I hope you can catch up, and we'll be wearing all black!
Azabel replied.   Bob and Saoirse arrive home,
with joy in their eyes.   Whats wrong? Lee asked.
Karen's going to become famous!   Said Bob.
"congrats!   Said Lee. As he shake Bobs hand.   The paper

CHAPTER : 36

Burn and vanished, It was weird! Said Saoirse. We have to
keep our eyes open". Said Lee.

A-while a go back, Jessica and Tasha was no-longer in
New-york. As they are flying in the sky, On the Horse.
Suddenly, purple thunder struck the Horse in the neck
and they tumbles down and land in a pool of Jello.
"Grape is my favorite! Said Tasha. As she start
eating the Jello. Jessica try climbing out the Jello, but
the jello stick to her body. " Seem like we're stuck! Said Jessica.
"You cant climb out, You have to eat your way out!
said Tasha. "What a great idea! Said Jessica and she
start eating the Jello. After five hr's of eating the Jello,

Tasha and Jessica was finally free. What a strange looking
place. Said Tasha. As the trees and sky was black and
purple, and so was the ground. This place doesn't
feel right". Said Tasha. I sense a wicked Wizzard.
Keep your eyes open. Said Jessica. As they start
walking through the woods. "I see you come into
my Kingdom! Said The voice of a man, with a
calm tone. Who are you and what do you want?
Jessica asked. All of a sudden, Jessicas Horse fall
out of the sky, and land infront of them.
When Jessica check on her Horse, it was long gone.

ha-ha ha ha ! He laughed. How could you hurt such
a beautiful animal?" asked Jessica.

Suddenly, a large tree come out of the ground,
holding axes. We should run across the wooden bridge!! shouted
Tasha. As she pull Jessicas hand and the tree chase after them.
there's no escaping from me! Said the tree.
As it throw one of its axes at them.

When they made it to the bridge, Jessica had no choice to
run across. As she hold onto the ropes. Tasha look
behind her and see the tree getting close and she does
the same. When Jessica look down, she see a river
with rocks in - between. " Dont look down, just keep
going!" Said Tasha. As she push Jessica forward.
Next, the bridge become wobbly. As the tree was
taking big steps towards them. When Tasha and Jessica made
off the bridge, Tasha pull a knife out of her back pocket
and start cutting the ropes. Jessica spread her

her arms and the ropes burn.
Before the tree takes one more step, the bridge tumbles
down. As the ropes snap”.
“Bye Bye Tree! Said Tasha. “where does this path lead
to? Jessica asked. As she follow the path. Wait for me!
Said Tasha. As she catch up with Jessica.

Karen was giving her own room and clothes,
to dress in for tonights show. Be ready for tonight!
Said Azabel. As she close the door behind her.
Karen put her clothes on the bed, and walk over to the
window. when she look out the window,
she can see the view of the city. All of a sudden..
The smell of food approach her nose, and she look to the
left and saw a table with food on it. So she walk away
from the window, to approach the table. when she carried off to
the table, there was Ham, Turkey, and chicken.
So she sit happily at the table and start eating”.

At night Karen fell-sleep on a full stomach, as Azabel enter into
her room and saw her sleeping. Suddenly,

Azabel levitate the bed and Karen woke up.
{The path lead to a castle
and it was surrounded by purple lions.   How we supposed
 to get pass? Tasha asked . "they're afraid of fire!
Said Jessica. As two swords appear in her hands.
You had powers all this time??   Tasha asked. You cant
use powers for everything .. it become' boring!   Said
Jessica.   All that running". Said Tasha.
"You finally made it to my castle! Said the evil wizzard.
As the lions guard him. I give you credit,
its pretty sharp! Said Tasha.   Now   you are   about
to die, with a compliment! Said the Wizzard. You killed
my Horse! Said Jessica. Attack!!!   shouted the Wizzard.
The Lions charge at them, in full speed.
Point your sword forward! Jessica said. Tasha
point her sword forward and a fire Bear appear
and it attack the lions and Vanish.
The wizzard grab Tasha and   fall-back to his position.

"You hide behind my best-friend? Jessica asked. Come closer
and I'll kill her!!" Shouted the Wizzard.   Suddenly, Tasha
stomp his feet and stab him in the heart.

The wizzard   turn into a purple stone, and
 it crumbles.   How we supposed to get out of here?   Tasha   asked.
As she turn away and fold her arms.   We   have to fly
out of here!   Said Jessica.   I dont suppose that!
Tasha said.   Things happen for a reason!   Jessica replied.
All of a sudden..   a   gallop   runs   out of the
the castle   and slides. " you're very beautiful!
Tasha said.   As she rub the horse chest.
"We can get out of here, now!   Said Jessica.
I think not! Said Tasha.   As she climbed   onto   the Horse.
we're in this together!   Said Jessica.
"I thank you for saving me But my journey is my own!".
Said Tasha.   Staring off into the distance.
Friends dont leave friends!
Said Jessica.   Good-bye, Jessica! Said Tasha.
As the gallop   spread its wings and fly into the
sky. Shouldnt have rescued her! Said
Jessica.   As she walk down the castle trail

Azabel book a limo service and was transport for tonight event.
Fans scream, as they walk down the aisle and Karen gives
them a hug.   Suddenly, one of the girls

CHAPTER : 37

Grab Karen by the arm and rushed through the entrance.
Azabel let' down her hair, before walking on stage.
As the Girls did the same. the music starts playing
and Azabel walk on-stage and start singing. While the
Girls dance in the back-ground.
Karen tried to blend in and the show was over.
Azabel and the Girls bow
and walk. off the stage. Leaving Karen behind. Karen
walk off stage and they was nowhere to be seen.
Where are you guys? Karen asked. As she search for them.
 they're on
different paths, and dont want you any'more. Said the Jewish
man, and he wears glasses. Did I do something wrong? Karen asked.
You can either go home or become huge? Said the Jewish
man. As a contract appear in his hand. Who are you?
Karen asked. My name is Do-fire". Said Do-fire.
What do I have to do? Karen replied. Sign your name
with your finger, and you'll be famous!" Said Do-fire.
Karen put her finger on the contract and sign her name.
The contract turned into blood. Next, they teleports from the back
stage and to the church parking lot. Where are we?
Karen asked. "you're home! Said Patrick. As he walk
towards her and blow dust in her face. Karen woke
up infront of a mirror and her hair was

orange.   What happened to my hair? She asked. You have to
252

look beautiful for the video! Said Do-fire.   As he snap his finger
and   Monks appear, holding video cameras.
Karen wears a short red dress and an Egyptian crown.
Action! Shouted Do-fire.   "Hey look, Its Karen!
Shouted Bob.   As he turn up the tv volume.   Everyone gathered
in the living room to watch karen dance and sing on tv.
as the monks was standing in the background.
This is awful! Said Lee.   What do you mean?
Bob asked.   Suddenly, the tv explode and Bob fall
onto the floor.   Drew and Saoirse help him off the floor.
That has never happened before!!   said Bob.   I have to
save her. Said Lee. "she's fine!   Said Bob. I wish I
could say the same, but she isnt!   Said Lee.

After the video, the monks throw her into
the cafe.   Take this pill, and make sure you
drink it down!!   shouted Patrick.   Karen swollow the pill and drink
it down.   After drinking it down, she become dizzy and
fall'-asleep.   "you're never going home! Said Patrick.
As he walk away. {Lee explain' about the danger that
Karen was in and Bob become sad.   Cant you bring
her home?!   Bob asked. }
I see what I can do. Said Lee. As he walk out the front
door.   Wait, Im coming with you!!" Shouted Saoirse.

as her and Lee jump on the mo-bike   and drive off in the distance.
they'll get her back, mr Bob!   Said Drew.

{two monks standing out-side talking,   until both of them was
 struck by lightning. Lee and Saoirse dress themselves in a
hurry proceeding   through the entrance and into the main
hall. there're only four halls!   Said Saoirse.   Lets take the
middle hall. Said Lee.   As he follow the smell of food.
As him and Saoirse walk through the hall,   the
wall was decorated with demonic paintings, and faces of
Patrick.   When they arrive at the cafe, Karen was
sleeping.   Hope shes alright!   Saoirse said.
You stay here, and I'll go talk to her. Said Lee.
As he act like a monk and approach the table.
Next, he sit at the table and tap Karen on the arm.
Its me, Leeporder". Said Lee. Karen open her eyes
and smiles and lay her head back down.   Suddenly,
Lee look around and put his hand on her head and
remove it. Not long,

Karen was healed and she lifted her head.
Im here to get you out of here".. Said Lee.
What should I do? Karen asked.   Follow my lead.

said Lee.   As him and Karen walk out together.

When Lee, Karen, and Saoirse made it into
the hall, the three of them rush out the entrance of the
church.   Saoirse threw off the robe and jump on the
mo-bike.   As Karen get on back of the bike.   We cant take her
home. Take her far as you can , and I'll catch up.
Said Lee. { Knowing it was too risky for her safe'ty.}
Karen hold onto Saoirse and they ride off into the distance.
Enter the kingdom, you die!   Said Do-fire. With his
brothers   beside him.
You dont own her soul!   Said Lee. As golden wings appear
on his back and his eyes like the rain and thunder,
with his body covered in   light.
Three of the jewish   men turn into
a jewish monster with three heads and wears a jewish
robe.   Lee punch a hole in their body
and fly' off into the distance   The jewish men vomit blood
and fall' forward, Leaving them to die.

{Patrick and   the Monks arrive to see , she has
gone.   Where is she?!! Patrick shouted.   we   thought
the Monks walk her out of here! Said a man
with black hair. Someone was here. Said one of the Monks}

I'll give you the powers to ride out and hunt them!
Said Patrick. Staring at them with the hands
behind the back.
Suddenly, the students stand up and their uniforms
has changed black. with black eyes blue.
Lets hunt! Said Patrick. Leading them out of the cafe.

{ Saoirse and Karen hide in the Hotel room. As Saoirse hid
the bike on the side of the building.
Karen sit in the bed and Saoirse sat by the window.
I hope Lee's okay! Said Karen.
He has the power to take care of him'self!   Said Saoirse.
Lee walk up to the door and knocked {on it}
Saoirse peek out the window, she see Lee at the door.
"It's Lee! Saoirse said. Karen get out of bed and open
the door. Hope the party isnt over! Said Lee.
As he close the door and sit in the chair.   What do we do
now? Karen asked. rest here, and leave the next day. Lee replied.
we can take her home, right? Saoirse asked.
they'll find her and cause so much death and pain!
they'll never stop, until I destroy them! Said Lee.
"Thank you for saving me! Said Karen.   Get some rest!
Said Lee. As he close his eyes to regain his powers.
Come out Karen, I know you're in there!!!" Shouted
Patrick. Karen sits up.   Let me handle this. Said Lee.
As he get up and walk out of the door.
Who might you be? Patrick asked. My name's Leeporder!
Said Lee. "Her soul belongs to my father!   Said Patrick.

CHAPTER : 38

your father dont own her". Said Lee. her
name's written in blood..!" Said Patrick. The students in the
back-ground start laughing. Lets go somewhere and battle
for her! said Lee. Are you mad? Asked Patrick. With a smirk".
Karen and Saoirse, come running out of the room. The students
frowns at Karen. Lets leave away from this place!
Said Patrick. As the owner was looking out the window.
Lee spread his wings and fly off into the sky.

Patrick and the students, did the same. Why are they leaving?
Karen asked.   I think Lee and that man's gonna fight!
Said Saoirse. As she start' the mo-bike and Karen jump
on back. the students surrounds
Lee and Patrick. "What's the rules Porder? Patrick asked.
First person to hit the ground, three times wins.
Lee replied. Thats easy. Said Patrick. As he kick Lee in
the chest and his body hit the ground.   Lee fly
off the ground. Not bad!   Said Lee. As he throw
multiple punches at Patrick.   Patrick catch Lee'
fist and flip him over and Lee body hit the ground again.
One more strike and she's mine!   Said Patrick.
Lee fly off the ground again.   Stay down, porder!

Said one of the students.   "Any last words? Asked Patrick.
"Yes! Said Lee.   As he fly and kick Patrick in the
stomach and the students   ambush Lee.
Thats not fair!"   Said Karen. Suddenly, the cloud open
and out rush   the white knights, attacking the students.

Lee kick Patrick to the ground. "Just couldnt play fair!
Said Lee. Patrick throw off his jacket and charge at
Lee. Lee flip Patrick over and kick him in the back
of the head. Karen and Saoirse smiles from below.

Suddenly, Patrick turn into a beast with two feet,
with a slender body and dog head. Saoirse and
Karen becomes shocked. "You dont put fear in me!
Said Lee. As he fly and kick" Patrick in the head,
and back kick" him again. Patrick perform a spining
evo and "strike" Lee in the face. The white knights
strike" the students down, with their swords. Patrick was
strike down, with the power of Leeporder.

they're too dangerous to be left in this world! Said the white
Knight. As he approach Lee. But, it'll hurt them!
Lee replied. You cant focus on how they will feel.
You have to focus on what's right for them.! Said the Knight.
Lee feet touch the ground. Karen and Saoirse
comes running. Is it over?? Karen asked. Take Karen home!
Said Lee. you're coming right? Saoirse asked.
I cant come! Lee said. As his body light up
and a gold light circle around him. Karen and Saoirse
eyes was full of tears and they both hugs him. They
have rejoined! Said the white Knight. Karen kiss Lee on

the lips and walk   away with Saoirse.   Lee smiles.

259

as he watch them get on the mo-bike and drive away
into the distance.   After   they was out of sight,   he
rejoin   the white-Knight's.   first I was going easy!!
But now the students and I - are drawing blood!!!"   Shouted
Patrick. "Come and get some!   Said Lee.   Attack!!
shouted Patrick.   As they charge at Lee and the white
Knights.   "Ready guys? Asked Lee.   White! White!! white!!
white!!   the Knights shouted. Holding up their swords.

 Lee and the knights charge at Patrick and the students.
.Before Lee   destroy them, he had flash-back memory of
Julie, Heather, and the team.   Second, meeting Karen,
saoirse, and drew. Suddenly, he throw a straight punch
that was so powerful… the earth shakes.

As Pitts was destroy.   Saoirse keeps the mo-bike steady.
As the road was shaking. Nothing was left But
the darkness and sky. Karen look back and back
at the road… with her heart dropping to her stomach.
It seem so unreal to her, for a man to risk his life to save her!
{Bob and Drew, sat on the porch playing cards until..
a sound of a mo-bike, at full speed, approach their ears.
Drew and Bob stand up at the same time , to
only see Karen and Saoirse coming down the road.
Its my sister, and Karen!!" shouted Drew. As he wave
at them. Bob was full of tears. As he see' Karen
on the back of the mo-bike.   Next, Bob run   off the porch
and hug Karen.   As they arrive on the grass.

WHAT THE FUTURE HOLDS FOR THEM!

Ready to go? Asked Saoirse. where's Lee? Drew asked.
He had to go on a long trip! Saoirse replied. As she
look off into the distance. You guys are leaving now?
Bob asked. We have to go home. Said Saoirse.
As Drew get on the back of the mo-bike. "I thank you
all for everything! Said Karen.
As she hug Drew and Saoirse. where's Lee? Bob asked.
Taking a long trip! Said Saoirse. As she start the
Mo-bike. Wait, This belong to them! Said Drew.
take it, It's yours! Said Bob. Thank you!
Said Saoirse. As she drive off into the distance.

I thought I was gonna lose you! Bob said. Leeporder saved
me! said Karen. That he did... And he told me he would!
I thank him from my heart! Said Bob. With his arm
around Karen. Suddenly, fire-works set off into the sky
and the people of the city shouted…. "Happy new-year!!!"
Karen and Bob sits on the porch to watch the fire-works.
Leaving Karen in memory of kissing Lee .

{Saoirse, and Drews journey wasnt over. As they take the
Journey to London england. Gabe won at the Casino and
him, Heather and the rest went shopping. Jessica turned
the evil wizzards kingdom, into her home.   Joana and
Law, took the same Journey as Saoirse and Drew.
As for Malisa, she finally made it out of her home
town and took the train to pennsylvania.   as for
Lee, "im sure he's out there somewhere, Putting emotions
into other hearts and teaching them how they can have their own
journey as well!
"Some see the moon different and some see the moon as
Paranormal!

THE END

be sure to look out for my brother, who's an artist. His name's... Brian Art!

www.ingramcontent.com/pod-product-compliance
Lightning Source LLC
Chambersburg PA
CBHW080713120726
48001CB00010B/2997